DATE DUE		

SHADOWS OF
A CHILDHOOD

SHADOWS OF A CHILDHOOD

A Novel of War and Friendship

ELISABETH GILLE

Translated from the French by Linda Coverdale

THE NEW PRESS

NEW YORK

LIBRARY OF CONGRESS
CATALOGING-IN-PUBLICATION DATA

Gille, Elisabeth
[Paysage de cendres. English]
Shadows of a childhood: a novel of war and friendship / Elisabeth Gille; translated from the French by Linda Coverdale.
p. cm.
ISBN 1-56584-388-6
I. Coverdale, Linda. II. Title.
PQ2667.I395P3913 1998
813'.914—dc21 97-27308

PUBLISHED IN THE UNITED STATES BY THE NEW PRESS, NEW YORK
DISTRIBUTED BY W. W. NORTON AND COMPANY, INC., NEW YORK

The New Press was established in 1990 as a not-for-profit alternative to the large, commercial publishing houses currently dominating the book publishing industry.

The New Press operates in the public interest rather than for private gain, and is committed to publishing, in innovative ways, works of educational, cultural, and community value that might not normally be commercially viable.

The New Press's offices are located at the City University of New York.

PRODUCTION MANAGEMENT BY KIM WAYMER

PRINTED IN THE UNITED STATES OF AMERICA

9 8 7 6 5 4 3 2 1

For Odile

PART ONE

CHAPTER I

"No," said Léa.

In the faint glow of the night light, a giant shadow climbed the wall behind her and leaned out across the ceiling with bristling black fangs. Trampled clothing rustled grimly at her feet. There was the sound of muted scuffling, and a noise like the rubbing of cardboard boxes. Something metallic banged jerkily against a hard surface. Little wooden balls clacked and crackled like gunfire. A slavering pack was licking at her thighs, snapping at her knees.

During the struggle, the flashlight beam pointed at Léa's lower body wobbled and suddenly shone directly into her face, a small olive and crimson ball bobbing on an ocean of winged coifs. Standing on the bed, she clutched her doll in her left hand and with her right, firmly clamped to her tummy the lace-trimmed slip that three nuns, bending over her in long dark habits with rosaries at their belts, were trying to wrestle off her. Bedsprings squeaked somewhere in the slumbering dormitory, and one little girl, disturbed at her dreams, let out a moan.

"Come now, my child, don't make such a fuss," whispered a voice.

But Léa fought on silently, fiercely. The doll slid into the crook of her arm. She hoisted it up firmly beneath her chin, and the vivid pink skull with its sparse blond tresses seemed to nestle at her neck. One of her attackers now succeeded in lifting up the slip, uncovering plump thighs and a pair of panties stretched so tightly over Léa's chubby belly that the elastic waistband had slipped below her navel. Another assailant grabbed one leg and forcibly raised the foot in an attempt to remove a shoe. Thrown off balance, Léa managed to brace herself against the head of the iron bed frame, but the nun's dangling rosary caught on the child's shoe buckle, pitching her onto the blanket. She scrambled furiously back to her feet, and stamping on the bedclothes, shrieked in a voice surprisingly loud for her size, "I'm cold!"

The flashlight beam dropped, and the huge, misshapen blotch spread out once again across the wall. On the twenty beds that filled the long room in two parallel rows, covers were pushed back, revealing tousle-headed girls who rolled over onto one elbow or sat up, rubbing their eyes. Startled and bewildered by that monstrous, writhing shadow, several children burst into tears. As though touched by contagion, others began to whimper, and soon the darkness of the dormitory swelled with wailing. Silent once more, Léa triumphantly surveyed the ravaged battlefield. The coifs bending low around her fluttered up again.

"We might as well turn on the light," sighed the nun with the flashlight.

"We can't do that, Sister Saint-Gabriel. What about the curfew?"

"Let's just hope the black-out paint on the windows is good and thick, or we'll get another visit from the air-raid warden."

On the second-to-last bed in the row, in the meager light of a bare bulb hanging from the ceiling, Léa stood revealed. Her curly hair looked like a mat of brown wool. Her dark cheeks were flushed with exertion and her small face contorted with rage. In the dim light, her flashing eyes seemed deep-set beneath their knitted brows. Standing like that among those beds with their pale blankets, she resembled a black nettle stuck into a clump of white tulips. Still clasping her doll to her breast, she abandoned the defense of her slip and popped her right thumb into her mouth. The shadow had shrunk to more normal dimensions. The sobbing died away, and all eyes turned inquisitively to Léa. Heads leaned close together; there was murmuring, and relieved laughter. The nuns stepped back.

With a starchy rustle and the clicking of beads, Sister Saint-Gabriel strode to the middle of the dormitory. She was a tall woman with black eyebrows and a Mediterranean complexion.

"Don't be frightened, my children," she said gently. "Here is a newcomer who has arrived in the middle of the night because her train was delayed, that's all. We'll introduce you tomorrow. For the moment, I'll tell you that her name is Léa and she's five years old." Turning toward the child, she added, "Come, dear. You must put on a nightgown."

But Léa refused to give in and held herself so rigid with determination that her legs trembled. Fearing that her tired eyes might close, she opened them wide and gazed in disbelief around the room at the painted windows, the bedsteads with their iron bars, and the three penguins (two skinny, one short and fat) with faces framed by white wings. Her eyes fell at last upon the bed directly across the aisle: sitting up in it was a girl with very black hair who looked a year or two older than Léa and stared back at her with big blue eyes fringed by dark lashes. When she was sure she had Léa's attention, she turned sideways, holding out one hand and placing her other hand on top of it in a fist. Then she wiggled her index and middle fingers in a scissoring motion. A duck appeared on the white wall, opening and closing its beak. The diminutive magician twisted around, winked, and smiled.

Speechless, Léa lowered the arm holding her doll, and her thumb slipped from her open mouth, trailing a thread of saliva. Seeing her chance, a nun went over, delicately pried open the child's fingers, placed the doll by her side, and swiftly peeled the slip off over her head. Léa's curls reappeared only to vanish again beneath the ample folds of a white nightgown edged with red ribbon. Her panties were whisked away, followed by her shoes and socks, and the child let herself be put to bed without further protest. Her gaze remained fixed on the opposite wall. A rabbit with large, quivering ears had just replaced the duck. The tall nun finally noticed what was going on.

"Bénédicte," she said, placing a towel and washcloth at the foot of Léa's bed, "tomorrow you will take care of our little newcomer. You will show her where the washroom is, help her get dressed, accompany her to the courtyard and then to the dining hall. And now, everyone go to sleep."

The light was turned out. The children lay back in their beds. The nuns tucked several of them in, made the sign of the cross with their thumbs on a few foreheads, and left the room. The night monitor, Sister Geneviève, returned to her cell, a space at the other end of the dormitory surrounded by white curtains on which her silhouette appeared, obese, as she removed her coif, tossing her head to flip back the long braids that tumbled down around her shoulders. Her beads rattled when she placed them on a chair. Fascinated by this new theater, Léa had slipped her thumb back into her mouth.

"If you keep that up, you'll get the mustard treatment tomorrow," whispered her neighbor to the left, who was lying on her side, watching Léa. "Or bitter aloes. That's even worse."

Léa looked at her, opened her mouth to start screaming again, but all at once fell asleep, vanquished, her fingers tangled in the doll's hair. There were more whispers, groans from straining bedsprings, the sound of a glass being set down on metal; then the dormitory sank into a deep sleep. After a few minutes of silence, through the closed windows came the distant tramping of hobnailed boots on pavement, the clatter of weapons, and the sound of humming, wafting on the night air. An order rang out, followed by a brief shout. There was a change in the rhythm of the sleepers' breathing, but no one stirred.

The other two nuns had remained out in the hall to listen, their ears pressed to the door. They straightened up, holding their backs.

"Is your brother still here, Sister Marthe?" asked Sister Saint-Gabriel.

"Yes. He's waiting for us in the kitchen, having something to eat."

"Let's go. He needs to rest awhile, and he'll have to leave as soon as curfew is over."

They gathered up the folds of their skirts, and with a hand on their beads to keep them still, went down the big stone staircase. On the ground-floor landing, the piled-up shoe cubbies where the children stored polish, rags, and brushes kept ghostly watch in the gleam of the flashlight. Another, smaller staircase, a wooden one this time, led down to the basement.

The vast kitchen was bathed in a darkness that stank of cabbage and rancid grease. Big cauldrons sat gaping on stoves with copper handles. Near a window covered with dark blue paper, a man wearing a beret was just finishing a meal by the light of a candle set in a saucer. He pulled off his beret, pushed away his plate, and stood up.

"She's asleep. It wasn't easy," said Sister Saint-Gabriel. "She seems a difficult child. Sit down, Monsieur Lombard, and tell us what happened."

The nuns drew up two chairs for themselves. Their coifs glinted in the half-light.

"A friend of ours at police headquarters was informed this morning that there was going to be a roundup. He has the list of all the Jews registered in Bordeaux. He went personally to find the parents, who are of Russian nationality. Only the little girl is French. He tried to convince them to leave home and go hide somewhere else. They wouldn't listen to him. The husband kept saying he had no problems with the authorities, that he and his wife had been wearing the yellow star since July, that they weren't involved in politics. And even that they were Catholic. As I told my sister, they said they'd converted in '39. By this time, they must be in the camp at Mérignac."

"But what about the little girl?"

"The police came to pick up the whole family in the early afternoon. We'd had time to warn a girl in the OSE, the Jewish organization. She went to get the kid. The parents still didn't want to let her go. They didn't know about the new memorandum, the one authorizing the removal of children as well.

The girl had a hard time convincing them. Finally, when they heard the knock on the door downstairs, the mother gave in. The father hesitated, then handed over his daughter's papers. Our friend carried her away and hid with her in the apartment of a neighbor who had opened her door a crack to see what was going on. The woman let them stay there for half an hour, no more. That's how we wound up with her."

"And how did the child take all this?"

"She never stopped howling. We finally had to gag her with her scarf. Since I was supposed to make a delivery with my truck, they asked me to hide her under the seat and bring her to you. My sister had told me that we could come here in an emergency. The kid cried so much she fell asleep. Here are her papers. Don't leave them lying around. Her baptismal certificate is there."

Sister Saint-Gabriel glanced reproachfully at Sister Marthe, a short, swarthy woman, who stared straight ahead without saying a word.

"And her parents?" asked Sister Saint-Gabriel, leafing through the documents before she thrust them into the deep pocket of her robe. "What will happen to them?"

"Mérignac is supposed to be cleared out tomorrow. They organized this roundup because they didn't reach their quota of Jews set by the Germans. They're packing everyone off, it seems. To a suburb of Paris, in Drancy."

"And then?"

"That, no one knows. There's talk of labor camps somewhere in Poland."

"The child has no other relatives?"

"The parents told us that all the others—aunts, uncles, grandparents—had stayed in Paris and that they'd been picked up in July. Since then, they haven't had any news of them."

"All right, Monsieur Lombard. We'll keep the child as long as is necessary. Under a false name, obviously. This war won't last forever. Perhaps the parents will be able to come fetch her before it's over. Go get some rest, now. We've fixed up a camp bed for you in our Reverend Mother's office. Your sister will take you there. She'll wake you at six o'clock."

To avoid wearing out the battery, the nun did not turn on her flashlight, guiding herself back upstairs from the kitchen by running her fingertips along the wall, which at that hour of the night gave off a musty odor that caught the throat. Everything was rotting in this old building in Bordeaux. It was too close to the river: paint peeled off in great strips, revealing plaster stained green by saltpeter. Whole sections plummeted from the ceilings. The wooden floors were extremely damp and gave way in places beneath one's feet, which sank into the parquet as though into a mush of sawdust. The one advantage of this dilapidation was that the men from the Kommandantur who had visited the boarding school two weeks earlier had quickly given up any idea of requisitioning it. Sister Saint-Gabriel could still see their leader, a lieutenant, standing in her small office brandishing his whip and poking it, with a look of disgust, into a rip in the wallpaper that had immediately split from floor to ceiling.

Sleep was out of the question. Now that things had quieted down, she had to use these few moments of calm to try to think. What should they do with this child who had no presentable papers, no change of clothes, no money, no ration card? She went to her cell for her shawl, returning to stand on the threshold and breathe deeply of the chill night air. Antiaircraft searchlights crossed and recrossed their beams of white light in a sky that was empty and silent without the all too frequent rumble of the Fying Fortresses. Today, at least, there had been no alert, the only siren that of a boat that must have outfoxed the British, running the blockade to bring tin or rubber from Japan. Supplies for the Germans, of course. What with these ships hunted by the Allied bombers, the submarine base, the Saint-Jean railroad station nearby that was attacked regularly, and the Atlantic Wall of pillboxes and bunkers being constructed by the Todt Division of the SS, Bordeaux was suffering. The breeze lifted up one wing of Sister Saint-

Gabriel's coif, which she settled more firmly on her head. By the time this war was over, what would be left of her city?

Trying to soften the racket of her wooden soles on the paving stones, she crossed the courtyard. The chapel she entered was even more frigid than the rest of the buildings. They had given up attempting to heat it, even during services. It was too big, too bare, the ceiling was too high, and the sweating stone walls too damp. Stale smells of incense and bad candle wax lingered in the air. She shuddered at the sight of Christ on his cross, a simple cloth knotted about his loins. The bare knees—one straight, the other bent—and bright pink feet pierced by a huge nail from which dripped blackish blood made her feel sick. After a hasty genuflection and sign of the cross before the altar, she turned away from the rows of seats reserved for the congregation and went to sit on one of the small chairs where the boarding students sat bundled up during Mass or Vespers.

What would the chaplain think of what she had done, if she were to tell him about it? And his superior, Monseigneur Feltin, Archbishop of Bordeaux—what would he say? Certain bishops had publicly condemned the persecution of Jews. Not he. He had given no directions, either in his sermons at the cathedral or in the parish bulletins. In the absence of the mother superior, trapped in Canada by the outbreak of the war, Sister Saint-Gabriel was the senior figure here, and thus the only one in charge. She had reacted instinctively to Sister Marthe's breathless news that her brother had just turned up at their door with a little girl asleep in his arms—a brother who had gone underground to avoid compulsory labor and who appeared at the convent from time to time at night, in the course of what were obviously clandestine missions. Sister Saint-Gabriel had known of this for quite a while, even if she had never said anything about it. Some of the nuns had fathers and cousins who were in England, or prisoners in Germany, or even members of one of the many militias in the service of Vichy. How could Léa's identity be kept secret? It would be better to conceal it from everyone except Sister Marthe, who already knew about her, and Sister Geneviève, who probably had her suspicions.

The child was baptized, of course. But what about this baptism? A Jewish family of Russian origin, converted in 1939, a few months before the declaration of war . . . Sister Saint-Gabriel touched the papers at the bottom of her pocket. After all, why not take Léa to police headquarters? She could rejoin her parents at the camp in Mérignac before they left for Drancy. Wasn't it cruel to separate her from them? This recent decision by the authorities to let the children go with their families—hadn't it been made out of generosity? Poland was supposed to be a very Catholic country: the Jews would probably be well treated there. Yet wasn't France, the eldest daughter of the Church, behaving most uncharitably toward foreigners now? Witness the series of roundups that had begun with that spectacular one on July 15. And the signs saying "No dogs or Jews allowed" that had sprung up everywhere after first appearing on the windows of Le Régent, a café on the Place Gambetta. In any case, how could they take the child to the police station without having to explain her arrival at the convent, thereby betraying her savior?

Sister Saint-Gabriel tried to pray. Her heart wasn't in it, and besides, she was tired. She rose, pulling her shawl more tightly around her shoulders. Outside, a murky dawn made the scrawny trees, skeletal flagpole, and uneven paving stones of the courtyard look even more wretched. The corrugated iron roof over the walkway stood out starkly against the milky white of a sky no longer lit up by anti-aircraft searchlights. She was too exhausted to think. She still had to find a uniform that would fit Léa, so that when the little girl dressed in the morning, she would look just like all the others. That is, if the convent decided to keep her. Luckily, in these times of scarcity, if there weren't any younger sisters at home to inherit the hand-me-downs, the mothers sometimes agreed to leave their daughters' outgrown uniforms at the school for poorer children to use. Sister Saint-Gabriel entered the storeroom and turned on the light. At that hour, even the volunteer air-raid wardens were probably asleep. Rummaging through boxes, she came up with some underwear, a skirt, a sweater, and a navy blue coat, which all seemed about the right size.

She returned to the peaceful dormitory, first removing her shoes and rosary before entering the room, which she crossed on tiptoes, pointing her flashlight at the floor. At Léa's bedside, she noticed that the child's hand had released its grip on the doll's hair and was lying on the covers, palm up, like a seashell. The nun gently removed the doll, then exchanged the clothes she had brought for Léa's things. The child's initials were delicately embroidered on the lace-trimmed slip. Frowning in amazement, Sister Saint-Gabriel felt the soft, smooth material that slid so easily through her fingers. Silk? She gathered up the plaid dress of fine wool with its puff sleeves and little white piqué collar, and the black patent leather Mary Janes. She had to get rid of these expensive things right away. And then Léa would have to be persuaded to answer to a different name, so that all trace of her origins would be gone. The child slept on, for the moment, with her thumb still in her mouth. It was hardly surprising, after all she'd been through, that she had behaved so badly. She would be calmer in the morning. At that age, they forgot quickly.

As for herself, there was no question of going back to bed. Soon it would be time for Matins. Sister Saint-Gabriel went back down to the kitchen, where pale light was already filtering through the gaps between poorly glued sheets of paper, and raised the lid on one of the stoves. The fire was laid. She threw a lighted match onto the pile of crumpled papers and carefully interlaced twigs, then fanned the tiny flame with a bellows. Next she placed on top a few pieces of coal taken from the scuttle, which was sparingly stocked each evening. When the fire was hot enough, she threw in the clothing, and without hesitation, the doll: the hair crackled and the face, warping in the heat, melted away with a grimace. First one, then the other glass eye shot from its orbit with a sound like a popping cork and ricocheted off the sides of the stove. Using tongs, Sister Saint-Gabriel fished both eyes out and buried them at the bottom of the garbage bin. Then she stirred up the fire once again. That evening she would rake out the ashes herself to make sure there was no clue left that could arouse suspicion. After Matins, when the nuns came in for breakfast, she would claim she'd had insomnia, to explain why she had lit the fire herself instead of leaving it to the sister whose duty this was. She looked around one last time. Aside from the papers hidden at the very bottom of her pocket, nothing remained of what had once been Léa's identity.

CHAPTER II

Bénédicte's hand was on the new schoolgirl's arm, shaking her awake.

"Didn't you hear the bell?"

Still half asleep, the child snuggled back into the warmth of the bed, feeling around automatically for her doll.

"Sister Saint-Gabriel took her away from you," said Bénédicte. "Here we're not allowed to have toys in bed."

Wide awake now, Léa sat up and met the serious gaze of two big blue eyes.

"I want her."

"Come on, don't make trouble, you'll get her back for vacations. Time to wash yourself. We'll be late."

The older girl picked up the pile of clothing left folded on the blanket by the nun the previous evening: white cotton panties and undershirt, a pleated navy blue skirt, and a sweater of the same color with a celluloid collar attached by buttons. She set everything down on the floor, along with her own clothes. Then she helped Léa out of bed. The little girl's thumb had immediately rejoined her mouth, while her eyes remained fixed on Bénédicte, who smoothed out the lower sheet and drew the upper one taut, pulling it up over the pillow before skillfully tucking in the blanket without leaving a single wrinkle.

"Now we're going to go wash."

"I want my nanny," replied Léa, dancing on the freezing tile floor. "She's the one who washes me in the morning. Mama gives me my bath at night."

"You're a big girl. You don't need a nurse anymore. I'll help you. Come on, let's go."

Giving in, Léa held tightly to her guide's nightgown with one hand and followed her through the deserted dormitory, passing between two perfectly straight rows of beds that were separated from one another by small tables. The silence made the room seem even more huge, and the dim light from the single bulb left pockets of shadow everywhere. A few scratches showed as white streaks in the dark blue paint covering the panes of two tall, closed windows, between which hung a large wooden crucifix. The little girls' breath floated in tiny puffs of vapor in the stagnant air.

They went by the silent curtains of the dorm monitor's cell and into the washroom next door, where a long table held two rows of basins. Pitchers of steaming water were poured into the basins, from which rose a cloying odor of cheap soap. Fat Sister Geneviève, clothed from head to toe in her long black habit and white-winged coif, supervised the girls' ablutions while telling her beads. Her charges in their identical nightgowns bent over water scummy with floating grayish lumps that stuck to the sides of the enameled basins. Washcloth or toothbrush in hand, everyone looked up or turned around, pushing back the hair falling into their eyes, to watch Léa enter the room.

"Hurry and wash yourself, Bénédicte. Léa, do as she does."

The older child poured boiling-hot water from a pitcher into several basins already half filled with cold water. She scrubbed her face, then slipped the washcloth beneath her nightgown and continued to wash herself like that from her armpits to her feet—somewhat hampered, however, by Léa's hand, which still clutched at her nightdress. The nun came to her rescue, opening the little fingers, and Léa, absorbed in what was going on around her, took hold of her own nightgown without thinking and made as if to pull it off over her head. The other girls all giggled and squealed in mock horror. The nun blushed.

"Here we wash and dress ourselves with modesty, Léa," she said. "We don't show our bodies to anyone, not even to our guardian angels . . ."

"Never mind, Sister," broke in Bénédicte. "I'm through, I'll show her how to do it, this time."

She lathered up the clean washcloth, crouched down, and

slipped it over Léa's hand, which she guided beneath the nightgown. The material was soon sticking clammily to the little girl's legs. The towel vanished in turn and more or less dried her off. Then Bénédicte demonstrated the acrobatics through which they managed to dress themselves without revealing one square inch of skin. You had to begin with the panties, which you stepped into, then pulled on with both hands without letting the nightgown ride up. After that, you went through contortions to wriggle your arms—one after the other and elbows first—out of your sleeves and inside the nightgown, into which you then withdrew your head. Thus blinded, you felt around for your sweater, which you put on in the shelter of this improvised tent. Next came the skirt. Then, and only then, you pulled off the nightgown.

Léa watched this bizarre performance in astonishment. Bénédicte put on her socks, tied her shoelaces, brushed her hair. Then she considered her motionless companion, shrugged, and began to dress her. Léa stood absolutely still, allowing her warm body to be manipulated like so much dead weight. The other girl stepped back to judge her work, straightened one point of the collar that kept curling up, then took her protégée by the hand and led her back into the dormitory, where the others were all waiting in a double line, dressed in the same navy blue uniforms. Standing in front of them, the nun flicked her clapper, and everyone filed downstairs. The last two, big nine-year-olds, turned around to look at the stragglers.

"She's so teensy, that new girl," remarked one of them. "Did you see her skirt? It droops down to her ankles. Poor Bénédicte—I hope you like playing nursemaid, 'cause this kid has latched on to you for good."

Coats were hanging on pegs in the narrow hall at the bottom of the stairs. Each girl took her own, and Bénédicte put the one that remained on Léa, along with a cap so big it came halfway down over her eyes.

A chilly wind swept in at the front door. Outside in the

courtyard, where the branches of four trees formed a tracery of inky black on a pearl-gray sky, the entire school had assembled around the flagpole. On one side, the compact square of nuns, their hands tucked into their sleeves. On the other, the shivering schoolgirls, at attention. One of them stepped forward and approached the flagpole.

"Today the Chamois team has the honor of raising the flag," announced Sister Saint-Gabriel, who stood before the formation of nuns like a captain at the prow of his ship. Turning around, she cried, "Children of France, always . . ."

"Ready!" replied a chorus of shrill voices.

The little girl pulled on a rope, and the blue, white, and red flag twitched its way up the pole. The clapper sounded.

"Maréchal, we are here . . ." began a nun.

And everyone joined in the song.

"Now, space yourselves out."

In perfect order, the girls divided up into parallel rows, holding their arms straight out at their sides until they touched their neighbors' fingertips, then making a quarter turn to repeat the operation, and facing front once again to begin their gymnastics session. Soles squeaked on the paving stones as the girls did jumping jacks. Bodies bent over and straightened up in cadence. The seats of panties appeared and disappeared to the rhythm of the clapper. Only Léa remained motionless, clutching the pleated skirt of her companion, who tried in vain to free herself so she could move about. Girls began nudging one another, turning around to look at them, and giggling uncontrollably. Bénédicte gave up with an imploring glance at the nun in charge. A blast on a whistle indicated it was time to form their double line and go quickly back inside.

Léa didn't let go of Bénédicte in the dining hall, either. She slipped in beside her at the tail end of a bench, one leg hanging off the side, until the others grudgingly moved over when a monitor told them to slide down. Talking was not allowed. They dunked their bread and margarine in a bowl of milk flavored with ersatz coffee while a student standing at a lectern up on a dais droned her way through the pages of a devotional text. It was hard to hear the reader's voice over the clinking of spoons and the constant murmuring that went up a notch in volume as soon as the monitor had passed by, brushing against the girls' backs as she went from table to table. Léa, who had not yet eaten anything, noticed that one of her neighbors was spreading jam on her bread. Taking her thumb from her mouth, Léa reached for the jam pot. With a scandalized expression, the other girl replaced the greaseproof paper cover on the jar and snapped a rubber band around it before putting the jam away, with proprietary care, next to a pâté, a hard sausage, and a piece of cheese nestled inside a small wooden box whose cover she then tightly closed. Eyebrows raised, the girls silently indicated their unanimous indignation at Léa's breach of etiquette. A fat blonde selected from her own box a jar of honey she then offered to her neighbor with a show of generosity. The gift was acknowledged with a pious smile before being whisked away.

"You're not allowed to touch their private treats," whispered Bénédicte. "You'll have to wait till your parents bring you your own."

When everyone had risen, given thanks, and lined up to leave the dining hall, the monitor came to get Léa. Seeing that she was about to be separated from Bénédicte, whose skirt she was still clutching, the child grabbed the corner of a table with her free hand and clung to it without a word. Two nuns hurried over, uncurled her fingers one by one, and picked her up bodily to carry her along staircases and corridors, shrieking and scarlet with anger. Flailing her rigid legs, Léa dealt the walls mighty kicks that knocked off chunks of plaster. The nuns bundled her along like that to Sister Saint-Gabriel's office, where they set her down on a chair and wiped their brows. Seizing this opening, Léa twisted around and, somewhat entangled in her skirt, tried to hop off her chair. Two hands grabbed her securely by the waist. Two more fell heavily on her shoulders.

"Calm down, my child," said Sister Saint-Gabriel. "You're behaving like a little savage. What would your dear parents say if they could see you?"

"My father will beat you up when he gets back from his trip," said Léa viciously.

"Until he does return, you must behave yourself. He has entrusted you to us, after all. I have sent for you to tell you certain things. Then you may rejoin your companions, who will welcome you like sisters."

"They don't want to give me their jam. I'll keep mine for Bénédicte and me when Mama brings me some. Where's my doll?"

"Playing with dolls is not allowed during the school year. Now, tell me. Do you know what your full name is? Is Léa the diminutive for Hélène? Éliane? Liliane?"

"My name is Léa Lévy and I live in Paris at 27 Boulevard des Invalides," the child replied all in one breath. "Mama's name is Alexandra. It's too long. Everyone calls her Assia. So she named me Léa so I'd always have the same one."

The nun sighed.

"Léa's fine. But your family name isn't right anymore. You'll have to learn a new one."

"Why?"

"Because your parents want you to."

"That's not true."

"They said so to the gentleman who brought you here last night. These are grown-up matters, something you wouldn't understand. But for as long as you will be here, your parents want you to be called Lelong. Léa Lelong. Or better yet, Éliane. You'll take back your old name when they come get you. That will be soon, you'll see. They must have gone off on a trip without taking you along. It would have been too tiring for a little girl your age. When they return, they'll be pleased to hear that you did as they asked."

Léa stared thoughtfully at the nun without replying.

"Do you think you might not be able to remember all this?"

The child laughed insolently.

"A-B-C-D-E-F-G-H-I-J-K-L-M-N-O-P-Q-R-S-T-U-V-W-X-Y-Z," she recited at top speed. "Papa says, 'My little girl's got the memory of an elephant.' "

"Well then, show him that he can be proud of you. And to please him, do try to be more obedient as well. You'll be learning lots of things in our boarding school. Since there are no other children of your age, I'm going to put you in a class of older girls. You'll learn to read and write. Think how happy your parents will be when they see you again."

"But I already know how to read," sniffed Léa disdainfully.

The nun smiled wanly. This child definitely had every fault: undisciplined, rude, proud, and a liar to boot. Boasting that she could read, at her age! She was going to be a handful. They would have to treat her gently, but firmly. Already so rebellious, at five years old! What kind of education had her parents spoiled her with? Her race was said to be overbearing and sly. Was it true, then? Sister Saint-Gabriel chided herself silently for being so uncharitable. Hadn't she just lied when she pretended to have received instructions from the child's family? A white lie. She would tell the chaplain about it during confession. No doubt she would have a wealth of opportunities to break the holy commandments. But what else could one do in these troubled times? As for the child, she was Jewish, true, but baptized. Perhaps she'd already begun to learn her catechism? In that case, things would be easier. Besides, upon closer examination, this tiny creature didn't seem so very dangerous: chubby, curly-haired, with her dimpled pink thighs showing beneath her hiked-up skirt, her whole thumb stuck in her mouth, dribbling saliva on her crooked collar (now missing a button)—she was obviously still just a baby. A baby who had already picked up some bad habits, but she could be molded, certainly. Sister Saint-Gabriel searched through her drawer for one of the rare candies, precious prewar souvenirs, that she doled out sparingly to the students as consolation for a skinned knee or in reward for a good grade. She held it out to Léa, who jumped off her chair and popped the sweet into her mouth.

"Sister Marthe, you will take our little newcomer to her class. Seat her next to Bénédicte. They seem to get on well together. She'll be a good influence on this child. Give Léa a notebook and a pencil. She'll be able to start practicing her letters during the older girls' lessons. In your spare time, prepare her to learn how to read. That way, at the end of the year, if she does well, we could plan on putting her in first grade."

Sister Marthe took Léa's hand, and this time the child did not resist. They had gone downstairs and were crossing the inner courtyard, passing by the main entrance, when someone pounded violently on the door outside. Sister Saint-Gabriel gathered up her skirt and came rushing down the steps, her white stockings showing beneath her hem, and after signaling behind her back for the other two to get quickly away, she pulled open the large copper bolt. A militiaman wearing a blue beret came in, revolver in hand, followed by two policemen dragging a man in torn clothes who was slumped over, his head hanging on his chest. Sister Marthe, who was leading Léa off toward the hallway, turned around, cried out, and dropped the child's hand.

"Pierre!"

"I see you recognize him," said the militiaman, grabbing the prisoner by his shirt collar and wrenching his chin up.

One eye was blackened, and blood trickled from his nose, which was swollen to twice normal size. Teeth were missing from a mouth that was now simply an open wound. Only the policemen's grip kept the man's broken body, reeking of sweat and fear, from collapsing at their feet.

"He's my brother."

"When did you see him last?"

"Early this morning. He spent the night in the convent."

"Why?"

"He was passing through Bordeaux. He came to see me.

Since it was too late for him to set out again before curfew, we invited him to sleep here. He left at dawn."

"And what brought him to our fair city?"

"He's a truck driver. He comes through Bordeaux about once a month. On this run, he told me he'd brought a load of boards from a sawmill in the Landes to a contractor in the harbor."

"Your brother's a Commie, didn't you know that? And probably a terrorist, too. He's transporting more than boards. We suspect him of trafficking in Yids. A few of them escaped the roundup yesterday. He wouldn't happen to have hidden them around here, by any chance?"

Sister Saint-Gabriel stepped forward.

"I would never have permitted that. We're all good citizens here and we respect the laws of Maréchal Pétain. If you wish to search the school, I will be happy to escort you."

"That's just fine, let's go." Then, noticing Léa watching them, he added, "You, for example, what's your name?"

Silence. Sister Saint-Gabriel began to speak.

"Let her answer. Well, what's your name?"

Léa, still sucking on her candy, tilted her head to one side and gave him a shrewd look.

"Léa Lelong," she replied, with a big smile that showed off her baby teeth, evenly spaced along pink gums.

"Léa?"

"That's the dinimative for Éliane. Mama said it was too hard for me to say when I was a baby. I used to say Léa. So that's why."

"And how come you're not in class?"

"I was naughty. They scolded me and took away my doll."

"All right. The policemen will wait here for me with the Yid smuggler. I'll go back to your class with you. I'm curious to see if all your classmates have names that are as French as yours."

The militiaman went over to Léa and ruffled her hair. She rubbed against his leg, laughing gaily. He gave her a little pat on the bottom to get her moving, but Sister Saint-Gabriel stepped quickly between them and led the way into the corridor, stopping at a wooden door with a small window in it. She knocked, entered the room, and announced, "Stand up, children."

A nun who had been pointing out some words on the blackboard to a pupil standing next to her now froze as the children got to their feet. Surprised by the silence, one girl, who'd had her head buried inside her desk, lowered the top and whimpered with fright before jamming her fist into her mouth and jumping up with the others.

"Sit down," said the militiaman. "Sister, don't let me disturb you. Go on with your work. I only want to see if your pupils do as well in French as in Yiddish."

"We're having a grammar lesson," stammered the nun. "We were studying the adjective and its characteristics in relation to the adverb. I'd asked Rose to give me the comparative forms of the adjective 'good' and the adverb 'well.' She seems to be having some difficulty remembering them," she added, with a strained little laugh that cracked at the end.

Rose, a girl of nine or ten with thin blond hair pulled to the side by a barrette, shifted mutely from one foot to the other, trying to hold back her tears. The entire class stared wide-eyed at the man's revolver as he toyed with it casually, rocking back and forth on his heels. Sister Saint-Gabriel had relaxed her grip on Léa's wrist, and the child now darted toward the blackboard. Realizing that she wasn't tall enough to reach it, she dragged a chair from the front row, maneuvered it with some difficulty over the edge of the dais, and clambered onto it. Stretching up on tiptoe, using chalk that screeched so horribly that it set the wincing officer's teeth on edge, she completed the exercise in her big, round handwriting. Next to "good" she wrote "bettor," then wrote it again next to "well."

Sister Saint-Gabriel took a step forward, clearing her throat nervously.

"Perfect, Léa. You still have some progress to make on your

spelling, but you've earned a good merit. Take the chair back to where you got it."

Léa tapped her foot.

"I don't want a good merit. Are you going to give me back my doll?"

Taken aback, the nun could only murmur, "We'll see."

"Stubborn as a mule!" exclaimed the officer. "Sister, you are to return her doll to her. That's an order. Now, you, put back that chair."

While Léa was doing this and returning to Sister Saint-Gabriel's side, the man glanced around at the other children, then went from desk to desk in a deathly silence, flipping their workbooks open to the first page to check their names. He did not notice that Léa had neither desk nor notebook. Finally he tucked his revolver into his belt, and clicking his heels, left the room.

CHAPTER III

Léa's first day at school was made even more trying by the problem of the doll, which Sister Saint-Gabriel would have been hard put to return. Backed into a corner, she tried to explain to the child that rules were rules, that toys were forbidden so as to avoid creating differences and arousing jealousy among the pupils. The little girl listened to this speech with fury in her eye.

"I'll look everywhere for her!" she screamed. "And I'll find her! That man will put you in prison if you don't obey him! And besides, she was a present from Papa. When he comes back tomorrow, he'll make you give her to me. He'll twist your arm until you show him the hiding place. He'll hurt you really bad!"

They had to send for Bénédicte, who had no trouble calming her down.

"I stopped playing with dolls a long time ago," she said placidly. "I think they're for babies. I'll teach you much nicer games if you'll be my friend."

That put an end to the matter, but Léa's character did not mellow during the next year and a half. For the most part, the other pupils were the daughters of businessmen, wine merchants, or men of property in Bordeaux. Their families regularly sent them the famous extras—butter, honey, jam—that they kept in carefully locked boxes, the keys to which they wore on golden chains around their necks, along with their religious medals or baptismal crosses. The first thing they did upon opening these boxes at mealtime was to verify the contents, which they shielded from sight with their arms while peering suspiciously under the raised lids. These provisions were used to trade, to seal alliances, to publicize quarrels. Treats were exchanged with smugly pious expressions, smiles of understanding, rapid glances around the table to size up the looks of envy and resentment. After closing the box again, you slipped the key officiously down the neck of your sweater. When thanks had been given at the end of the meal, you left the room with your arm draped around the neck of the lucky one to whom you'd just generously proven your friendship.

Léa was a hearty eater. She had to be content with the ration of milk and two casein cookies distributed during morning recess, occasionally augmented by a thin bar of vitamin-enriched chocolate. As for the menu at lunch and dinner, it consisted simply of lentils (which the girls had to pick over for tiny stones during their free time in the evening), rutabagas, and Jerusalem artichokes, sometimes served with the noodles and the hundred grams of meat that made up the weekly fare of the French population. And it all smelled disgustingly of some mysterious grease that had replaced butter and even margarine. Despite the cook's labors of imagination, which produced such desserts as pumpkin compote and custards made with colored gelatin, there was real hunger in the boarding school, just as there was everywhere else.

Like Léa, Bénédicte did not receive any extra treats, and she never left the school, either, even though the other girls spent their weekends and holidays with their families. When her classmates questioned her, Bénédicte replied that her parents were in America, that the war had caught them there by surprise, and that of course they couldn't send her either letters or packages. The others felt pity or disdain for this girl who, by her own admission, had no brothers or sisters, aunts or uncles, or even grandparents. As for Léa, no one asked her anything anymore, so tired were they of her eternal answer: "My mama and papa are off on a trip. They're very rich and very powerful. When they come back to get me, they're going to bring me lots of pretty things and they'll kill everyone who was mean to me." A declaration that had often been reported to the highest authority and for which Léa had been lectured and punished many times, but which she never varied.

In spite of the two-year difference in their ages, the friendship between Léa and Bénédicte grew ever stronger, and probably owed much to those solitary days spent together in the deserted school. When the last of the mothers—all dressed up in their tight-fitting suits, hats with veils perched on their permanent waves, fake crocodile purses in hand—had trotted off on their platform shoes with their offspring in tow, strange echoes filled the empty rooms, and the muffled steps of the nuns in their slippers swished along the tiled hallways. Discipline was relaxed, and Léa and Bénédicte could even avoid the triweekly Masses, either by managing to be forgotten or by hiding long enough so that the sister sent to find them gave up and dashed for the chapel in a flurry of skirts, terrified at the thought of missing the *Introit*. Or else they'd lose their berets on purpose at the last moment and be unable to enter the holy place without those indispensable accessories.

Instead of scraping their knees on the harsh straw of the prayer stools, they would lie on their stomachs on the same bed in the dormitory and read. Since the younger girl had quickly learned to read as well as the older one, they turned the pages together: old illustrated magazines with so many pages missing that they sometimes had to figure out the stories on their own; conservative Catholic Youth propaganda; volumes from a series of children's books, with tattered, taped-up covers; even the many lives of the saints for young readers that cluttered the school's meager bookshelves. With their legs in the air, they kicked their heels in the same rhythm. Now and then, out of mischief, when her friend was absorbed in her reading, Léa would slowly ease off one of Bénédicte's socks with her toes without getting caught. Once in possession of her trophy, she'd wriggle off the bed like an eel, run to the window, and threaten to toss the sock into the street. Bénédicte would then pounce on her, grabbing her by the waist to tickle her stomach. These tussles would end in hysterical laughter that left them sprawled on the floor, panting.

At meals, which they ate alone in the abandoned dining hall at the table closest to the kitchen, in an odor of rancid grease that seemed even more acrid than usual, talking was now allowed, a compensation of which they took full advantage, as they were both chatterboxes with endless things to say to each other. And they began to spend more and more time acting out scenes from imaginary plays. They had created roles for themselves taken from a book in the Catholic *Signposts* series: one became Prince Éric, the other his friend Christian. They went by these names in secret, whispering them into each other's ears or even saying them silently when they felt threatened with discovery. They spent hours inventing a secret alphabet so they could send each other messages, which they rolled up tightly and stuck into the cracks of their desks. They went so far as to correspond (by tapping their fingernails) in Morse code, the rudiments of which they'd learned from a scouts' manual.

On Monday mornings, they rubbed their eyes as though awakening from a dream when their classmates arrived in a boisterous crowd. And with their return came news of the war. In those years of '42 and '43, because of its strategic position, Bordeaux was under the enemy's heel, perhaps more so than any other occupied city. Hardly had the camp at Mérignac sent its occupants off to the railroad station in covered trucks, bound for Drancy or Pithiviers before beginning their last voyage, than more haggard throngs would arrive, many in coats marked with the yellow star. There were endless raids, punitive expeditions, mass arrests of Resistance members. The military fort at Hâ was never empty. All the girls had family and friends in the militia or the Resistance. They repeated things they'd heard around the dinner table at home, embellishing the stories with macabre details: corpses found with their throats cut, hostages who had been tortured, hanged, or shot. They stood about in little groups during recess with their arms around one another's waists, whispering these tales. The nuns tried in vain to put a stop to all this by breaking up these gatherings, which simply reappeared as soon as the sisters' backs were turned, and the gossiping would begin again, with knowing glances at the two girls who were always excluded from these councils. Sometimes Bénédicte would grow pale; even the blue of her eyes would seem to fade, and Léa would catch a glimpse in them of something bewildered and distraught. She was aching to question her, because she'd often heard the other girls speak doubtfully of the supposed trip to America, but with a wisdom far beyond her years, she held her tongue. Tugging on her friend's skirt to rouse her from this trance, Léa would show off her latest skills at jump rope or hopscotch.

And although the two girls flung themselves wholeheartedly into their make-believe world—especially during the days they spent alone, days that seemed suspended outside of time—they never mentioned the secrets of their real lives. They neither confided in nor lied to each other. Léa's boasting about her canopied four-poster bed in Paris, the gold faucets in the bathroom, her dresses and playthings (a dollhouse, tea sets, a box of beads for stringing necklaces) overwhelmed her provincial classmates, who listened open-mouthed, unable to keep themselves from believing just a bit in all these details. Yet Léa never spoke of them in front of Bénédicte. Neither did she show her the little notebook she hid beneath her pillow and in which she wrote down the things she would tell her mother and father when they returned: tricks played on the other girls, ripped up schoolwork, stolen candies, the bullying she'd had to endure, the hair-pulling, and insults like the nickname they were always calling her, "the Ivory Soap Baby," which really drove her wild.

For the maturity Léa demonstrated in her relations with Bénédicte was entirely missing from the rest of her life. In fact, her behavior was outrageous. She regularly received zero for conduct. She would climb on top of her desk in class, clowning around, flapping the eraser cloth over the heads of her neighbors, who would jump up squealing. With her hair every which way, her nose always smudged with violet ink, her smock torn, her collar crooked, she looked like a devil, and the nuns would stealthily cross themselves at the sight of her. She talked back to her teachers, let herself be dragged to the corner like a log, and would lie down on the floor, legs bent to display her underpants. Sister Saint-Gabriel would summon Léa to her office and scold her severely, but she could hardly threaten to show her parents her poor conduct reports. Nor could she take away her outside privileges, since Léa never left the school. After the stick, the nun often used the carrot, suggesting how pleased her parents would be to come back and find their little girl both older and wiser, but the good sister would be brought up short by a cool stare and the everlasting reply, "When my parents come back, they're going to kill you." After Léa had knelt and recited her rosary as punishment, reeling off the words like a drunken parrot, Sister Saint-Gabriel would send her away and sit gazing thoughtfully at the door she closed behind her. What was to be done with this uncontrollable child, for whom she was perhaps damning herself by feeding her with the other children's ration cards, for whom the nuns had painstakingly knitted birthday presents of a pair of gloves and some socks out of scraps of wool unraveled from a few shabby old sweaters, and who nevertheless had not shown one shred of gratitude? Not only that, but the rebellious child was constantly disappearing. She now knew the boarding school like the back of her hand and would vanish as if by magic to spend whole days hiding in a cupboard or off in some odd corner with a book. Bénédicte was the only one familiar with her hiding places, but she never betrayed her friend.

They had given up trying to make her join in certain activities. For example, the sessions of eurhythmics recommended by the Minister of Education, Abel Bonnard, as being more suitable for girls than athletics and more apt to develop their aesthetic sense and physical grace. In short tunics revealing legs that were too plump or too skinny, the students would lackadaisically wave around scarves of colored muslin while a nun at the piano tried to thump out the beat, and in the middle of it all would be Léa, mixing up her right and left, taking a step forward instead of backward—in short, fouling everything up.

She was even forbidden to sing in the choir: not only did she sing flat, but she did so with such confidence, and so loudly, that everyone wound up going off-key.

In the spring of 1943, however, soon after her sixth birthday, a serious problem arose. Should she be allowed to make her First Communion—or rather, encouraged to do so, since she expressed absolutely no interest in the idea? She knew her catechism by heart but never stopped asking questions that might have passed for provocations and blasphemies, coming from an older child. What was God doing during this war? Was he blind, or on vacation? If Christ was his son, why had he let him die? Coming out of nowhere in a piping little voice, her questions left the other students exclaiming in horror or choking with mirth. Making no attempt to answer her, the good sister in charge of the class would simply order her from the room, then do her best to quiet down a class Léa had a genius for disrupting. In addition to all her faults, the child strutted around as though she were the Queen of Sheba. In spite of her youth, the other girls were afraid of her: when she didn't strike back at her tormentors with mockery or nasty jokes, she had such violent temper tantrums that the nuns would panic, and punish those who had provoked them even more often than they deserved.

Her stubborn insistence on accompanying the other girls to the cathedral, where Monseigneur Feltin was to celebrate the feast of Joan of Arc with great pomp on May Day, was seen as a first flicker of interest in religion. There was some suspicion, naturally, that the real attraction was not so much the archbishop's sermon as it was the baskets the children would wear suspended from their necks by sky-blue ribbons and filled with rose petals to be strewn along the path of the procession, but in the end, the nuns gave in. Sister Saint-Germain secretly instructed Sister Marthe to hide Léa in the middle of all the girls and to keep an eye on her every single second. The nun was able to report afterward that the child had tossed her petals and sung her hymns with great enthusiasm—and for once, without drawing attention to herself through naughty or capricious behavior. She had trudged along a route that followed the course of the Marne all the way up to the Porte d'Aquitaine before entering the center of Bordeaux, where the narrow streets had been so gaily decorated that one no longer noticed the empty shop windows. She had not tried to run off as the procession had chanted litanies and followed its standard-bearer in a complete circuit of the Hôpital Saint-André, which had been discreetly emptied the day before, moreover, with complete disregard for the eleven elderly Jewish patients plucked from their beds and packed off to Mérignac. Together with students from other religious institutions, the girls had then watched the ceremony from seats in the front rows. Léa seemed as thrilled as everyone else by the purples and golds of the priests and their acolytes, by the clouds of incense and thundering organ music. On the way back, she paid the same attention to the officers in black uniforms laughing on the sidewalks, strolling along with revolvers at their waists and the double *S* stitched into their collars in silver thread.

It was decided to interpret her fascination as religious fervor and to opt for Communion: the Host could only strengthen her in those good intentions so generously attributed to her by the sisters. There remained the problem of what Léa would wear. After some thought, Sister Marthe took down a muslin curtain that she bleached and cut up to make a dress. A few mothers donated shoes, socks, and white gloves for the little refugee. Some sweetbrier roses from a garden provided the crown. "You look like a prune in a bowl of whipped cream," scoffed one of her enemies, who was punished on the spot. Léa enjoyed the ceremony all the more in that she was the only star of this show, since the other girls had already been confirmed a long while ago. She was pampered, she was congratulated, she was given presents (including a pencil box decorated with a picture of Maréchal Pétain's baton), and even though the day finally ended in disaster, it wasn't spoiled through any misbehavior this time, but because a wasp attracted by the flowers in Léa's crown promptly stung her on the forehead.

Taking advantage of a clear sky that night, the Allies deluged Bordeaux with bombs. Although the most damage was done some distance away, at the submarine base to the north of Les Quinconces, the Flying Fortresses had enough left in their bomb bays to give a good drenching to the Saint-Jean train station and the naval academy, which were both near the boarding school. This wasn't the first bombing raid they'd experienced—far from it. On the night in question, the planes arrived well after bedtime, and long after the girls had knelt at the foot of their beds to recite the prayer they had prudently been taught to say every evening, in case the convent should be buried without warning beneath bombs: "Dear Lord, if I should die before I wake, forgive me my sins and receive me into your blessed paradise."

The students had been told that as soon as they were awakened by air-raid sirens they were to wrap themselves in the blankets from their beds and leave the dormitory in an orderly fashion, each older girl holding the hand of a younger one. The worst part was crossing the courtyard to the shelter beneath a black sky streaked with white by the anti-aircraft searchlights and flushed with the brutal light of raging flames, in the din of explosions and the rumble of the bombers, a shuddering bass that turned to shrill screams when the fighters nose-dived over the city. Fires broke out everywhere. The air reeked of burning and explosives.

The line of students, like so many phantoms bundled in their pale blankets, vanished as though swallowed up by the earth, down stairs cut from the soil itself and edged with billets to keep them from collapsing. Everyone hurried to the back of the damp, narrow space as the creaking door of wooden planks was slammed shut behind them. Friends clustered together, and Léa naturally clung to Bénédicte. They sat on benches lined up along the walls of logs, or huddled on the chilly dirt floor, on flimsy scraps of canvas. While the nuns told their beads, reciting Hail Marys in trembling voices, Léa and Bénédicte embroidered the continuing saga of their imaginary lives. After escaping to London, Éric and Christian had parachuted into Occupied France. Captured, tortured in separate basement cells, they hadn't talked and were ready to swallow their cyanide pills to avoid betraying each other when they were saved at the last second by a bombing raid that destroyed the Kommandantur, killing everyone but them. They had fallen into one another's arms and set off immediately on new adventures.

That night, there had been plenty of time to create fresh episodes while they waited endlessly for the all-clear sirens. At one point, a series of deafening explosions battered their refuge so terrifically that some logs fell from the walls. Fissures appeared in the shaking ground. Smoke seeped into the shelter, making everyone cough. The nuns asked their flock to kneel, and then recited the prayer for the dead. *"De profundis, clamavi ad te, domine . . ."* In the absence of the chaplain, Sister Saint-Gabriel took it upon herself to bless them. One more breach of the rules of her order could hardly matter. Awed by the gravity of the moment, the children wailing for their mothers fell silent. Bénédicte drew Léa beneath her blanket, which she pulled over both their heads, and told her to close her eyes. Then the thunder died away, and the drone of the departing bombers reverberated through the shelter once again. When the all-clear sounded, no one dared believe it. There was a long silence, broken by shouting and fists pounding on the shelter door, which Sister Saint-Gabriel opened cautiously to find that neighbors had come to make sure the children and their teachers were still alive. As a special dispensation, she allowed her charges into the dining hall, where they were served, by candlelight, a concoction made from acorns and dandelions and sweetened with saccharin. She even went so far as to uncork a precious bottle of rum she'd been saving in her pharmacy for years, pouring a drop of it into each child's bowl. Reddened eyes peered from wan faces in the spectral, flickering light.

The next morning, the children were allowed to sleep later than usual. When Sister Marthe went to awaken them, she noticed that Léa and Bénédicte were missing. Wondering if they'd run off during the panic of the previous night, the nuns anxiously searched the school. The girls were found in the W.C., standing on the rim of the toilet bowl to peek out the tiny window. The building across the way had been hit dead-on by a bomb, and only one jagged wall remained. A torn curtain flapped in the wind outside the single unbroken window. A pile of debris reached halfway up the front door. Wisps of smoke were still rising from the ruins. Arms and legs protruded from the canvas flaps of a covered truck filled with corpses that was trying to make its way through all the rubble. Ambulance attendants wearing red crosses on their backs unfolded their stretchers. German officers observed the scene, slapping their whips against their boots. Bewildered old women picked numbly through the wreckage. One of them stood up, clutching a dented saucepan to her heart.

Sister Marthe tugged on the two girls' nightgowns to make them get down from their perch. Whirling around, they stared at her in surprise, as though reality had turned inside out overnight and this apparition in a long black habit and a coif concealing every last strand of hair were the eruption of something fantastic into a universe where catastrophe had become a commonplace of daily life. Clambering off the toilet, Léa and Bénédicte reached spontaneously for each other's hands. Not a word was said. Without scolding them, the nun simply pointed toward the dormitory and sent the girls on their way.

CHAPTER IV

The increasing number of air raids further emptied out the boarding school, which had not been very full in the first place. The local authorities strongly advised the evacuation of all children. Some girls left as a group for a château that had been requisitioned in the Vendée. Others returned home to their families. Was it possible to arrange for Léa's departure as well? Sister Marthe might have been able, in an emergency, to obtain false papers for her through some friends of her brother, Pierre, who seemed to have vanished without a trace. These friends, however, were disappearing in turn, so tightly was a deadly net closing around the Resistance, whose members were now frequently arrested, tortured, gunned down, and executed in Bordeaux and the surrounding area as a result of infiltrations, suspected betrayals, and their own recklessness. Sister Saint-Gabriel briefly considered trying to spirit Léa away when she learned that the police, under the orders of the Feldkommandantur, were relentlessly tracking down the last Jews in the city. Her heart stopped every time the bell rang at the front gate, and she had secretly prepared a hiding place in a cupboard, behind a loose panel, where she planned to conceal the child if worse came to worst.

After searching the hospitals, the authorities were now visiting nursing homes and in particular, all religious establishments, which had been closely watched and subject to endless harassment ever since the Grand Rabbi himself had narrowly escaped arrest and found refuge at the archbishop's residence. Sister Saint-Gabriel, who often found herself dreaming of the day when she would be rid of Léa, felt ashamed when she learned of this, and resolved to take care of the child at all costs, no matter how troublesome she was. If something were to happen to Léa outside the school, she would never forgive herself. Especially since there were alarming rumors about the fate of the deportees. People were beginning to wonder why they'd had no news of them from far-off Poland. Not one person in Bordeaux had received even so much as a single preprinted postcard listing every possible situation—"So-and-so is in good health/slightly/seriously ill/ wounded/deceased/a prisoner/has been killed (cross out all inapplicable information)"—and ending, as though the censor had momentarily faltered while thinking of the woman who would learn in these succinct terms that her son or husband was dead, with "Fond thoughts. Kisses." Although one of these messages would occasionally reach the family of a Resistance member, the Jews were shrouded in the deepest silence. And yet, people said, some information should have filtered out of even the harshest concentration camps, such as that Auschwitz with the unpronounceable name where Jews were sent with top priority. No one had ever heard of jailers inhuman enough to forbid even the sending and receiving of mail in a place of detention. Or if they had, the Red Cross would have intervened. It was simply mystifying.

One day the chaplain (to whom Sister Saint-Gabriel, perhaps more out of superstition than mistrust, had in the end said nothing about Léa and her true identity—and consequently nothing about the moral quandaries she found herself in through the child's presence) pulled Sister Saint-Gabriel aside after Mass and led her into the cloakroom he used as a sacristy.

"Your young pupil, little Léa, whose confession I've been hearing since preparing her for her First Communion—do you know, Sister, she worries me . . . I'm not betraying any secret by speaking of this. Not only does she never find herself guilty of a single sin, in spite of all my suggestions—no disobedience, not one fault of honesty or charity, not even an unkind thought—but she spends the weekly quarter of an hour I devote to her in the confessional talking to me about her parents, who are away, I believe. They're quite wealthy, she tells me?"

Stunned by the child's nerve, Sister Saint-Gabriel hid her dismay at Léa's rashness behind a fit of coughing and instantly decided both to keep the truth to herself and to spend the night on her knees in her cell as penance for her lie.

"She's a very imaginative child—too imaginative, perhaps, even though she thinks she never lies. Her parents are well-off shopkeepers, as far as I know, in Paris, and they pay her school fees regularly, but nothing beyond that. They sent her to us because they're so overwhelmed with problems in these difficult times that they can't take care of her properly after school, and of course they wish her to have a solid religious education. One of our former students recommended our school to them."

"I see," said the priest. "That explains it. Listening to her describe her life in Paris, I almost envisioned the showy apartment of one of those extremely rich Israelites who've brought misfortune down on the heads of their brothers. I will at least be able to rub her nose in the sin of vanity, if nothing else. Is she really so well behaved?"

"A mite undisciplined, at times; talkative, as you've no doubt noticed, but that's not surprising, given her youth. A good little heart, and truly pious since her First Communion. Question her some day on her catechism, you'll see."

Sister Saint-Gabriel knew she risked nothing with that suggestion. Simply offering Léa the chance to shine was the way to get anything at all from her—not only a complete run through the catechism, but a flawless listing of important cities and capitals, the multiplication tables, the major dates in French history, and every single poem she'd ever heard the big girls recite since her arrival in the school. Although her handwriting was poor and she treated her inkstained notebooks so badly that on several occasions they'd been pinned to her back in hopes that the other students, gathering around her during recess, might teach her some humility (they had made fun of her, in fact, but she'd spun around to face the mob, sticking her tongue out at them), still, it had to be said: Léa wasn't stupid.

What Sister Saint-Gabriel didn't realize was that these extravagant details about the child's former life were the result of her growing amnesia: the more memories she lost, the more she invented. She would never have admitted it, not even to Bénédicte, but her parents' faces were fading, no longer appearing to her except in snatches, as she was dropping off to sleep at night. She still saw them again sometimes, when her vigilance flagged and her eyelids drooped: her mother in an evening gown, dark-haired, radiant, and her father in a tuxedo, white shirtfront, and black bow tie, holding a cigar, and they would bend over her bed at home on the Boulevard des Invalides, while her fat, smiling nurse stood waiting behind them. As soon as she tried to hold them, they would slip away. She would shut her eyes tightly, trying to drive everything else from her head, but they wouldn't come back. Then she'd start sucking her thumb again, noisily, at the risk of infuriating her awakened neighbor. When she finally fell asleep, she always had the same dream: she'd be in the middle of a group of people crowded into a bare room. A glass light globe hanging from the ceiling by a chain would turn red, swinging back and forth, faster and faster, and with each pass, it would kill someone. Wriggling desperately through the thicket of grown-ups' legs, she would reach the door, only to find, once she'd managed to open it, a writhing snake hissing in her face.

It was on days following these nocturnal reminiscences and nightmares that she would launch into floods of detail about her mother's dresses, her father's car, the parties they gave in Paris. In front of adults, including the nuns, she even went back to dropping the clumsy little curtsies she'd made when she first arrived and which she'd abandoned in the face of the other girls' sarcasm.

Her companions felt even angrier with themselves for hanging on Léa's every word sometimes, because of the striking contrast between her description of her parents' elegant social life and the ridiculous spectacle of the child herself, haphazardly rigged out in smocks that were too big for her, cinched at the waist by a twisted belt and falling in uneven folds over socks that were always down around her ankles. And worst of all, Léa's hair was still completely unmanageable. At the weekly afternoon delousing sessions, held in the courtyard in good weather or under the walkway when it rained, she was put at the end of the line. Running the fine-toothed comb through the other girls' smooth hair was child's play compared to untangling that curly mop, full of snarls that were all the more matted since the nuns could never completely get rid of the nits, which meant that Léa was constantly scratching. When the rest of the students had returned to their games, the sister in charge would sigh deeply, seat Léa on a chair, drape a towel around her shoulders, and tackle the job, which lasted for hours. The victim fidgeted, wailed, covered her head with both hands, sniffled, and wept. The torturer began with the brush, moved on to the comb, then to the fine-toothed comb, snipping off the odd tangle on the sly. To quiet Léa by proving to her how necessary the procedure was, the nun would occasionally show her a particularly fat louse, held out between her thumb and index fingers. Then she would wash the child's curls with a product that stank of gasoline, apply a vinegar rinse, and sprinkle on Marie-Rose talc. Free at last but reeking and prematurely white-haired, wiping away her tears and snot with the backs of her dirty hands, Léa would go off to rejoin the others, who would dash a few yards away, gather in little groups, and chant, "Lousy Léa! Lousy Léa!" Even Bénédicte, who naturally never joined in the chorus, could not help shrinking back.

It was on an evening early in 1944 that Sister Marthe learned, through her contacts at the city hall, that the much dreaded search was imminent. That was enough to send Sister Saint-Gabriel racing to awaken Léa. The few remaining boarding students had been placed in a different dormitory, leaving only Léa and Bénédicte in their old one, in the event of such an emergency. The younger girl had just fallen asleep, and now, rubbing her eyes, she began to whimper. Alerted by the noise, her friend sat up in bed. The nun suddenly realized that it would be hard to explain the presence there of a single student after she'd hidden Léa away, and that the safest thing was to conceal them both. She might as well tell the truth to the older child, who had often demonstrated remarkable maturity, and ask her to help.

"Bénédicte," she said in a low voice. "The police are coming to search the school. They mustn't find Léa. I've fixed up a hiding place. She'll be less frightened if you go with her. Will you do it?"

The blue eyes solemnly acquiesced. The head of short black hair, so quick to fall sleekly back into place, gave a little nod. Bénédicte scrambled out of bed. Now fully awake, Léa followed her friend's lead by gathering up her bathrobe and slippers, but there was not enough time to put them on before Sister Saint-Gabriel, grabbing both their blankets and tucking them under her arm, hustled the girls out to the landing and down the stairs, as her flashlight sent pools of brightness rippling through the utter darkness. The stone steps were icy beneath their bare feet. The musty odor stung their noses. The walls and ceiling seemed to have withdrawn into a cave of silence.

To the nun's astonishment, Léa and Bénédicte sped directly to the cupboard she had prepared in such secrecy at the far end of the small storeroom. After putting on their robes and slippers, they climbed inside and settled on the eiderdown already tucked into the bottom of the closet. Sister Saint-Gabriel handed in the blankets, which they wrapped around themselves, and showed them the box of cookies, the dried figs, and the bottles of water she had placed there. Before closing the false panel, she shined the flashlight into their faces: staring back at her were two blue eyes, clear and calm, and two terrified black eyes beneath a mass of curls. Haughty Léa was just a six-year-old again. Realizing that they were to be left alone in the dark, the child looked as if she were going to cry. Bénédicte slipped her hand over her friend's mouth.

"Don't worry, Sister," she whispered. "I'll take care of her."

The nun made the sign of the cross on their foreheads.

"Pray, my children," she told them. "Your guardian angel will protect you."

After sliding the panel into place, she stood motionless for a few seconds, listening. Bénédicte's soft voice began to murmur.

"So Éric and Christian decided to go rescue their comrades, who were imprisoned in the Fort du Hâ. They both hid in the trunk of a German officer's car. The ride lasted a long time, but they had food and water . . ."

Sister Saint-Gabriel didn't listen any further, closed the cupboard, and ran back to the dormitory, where she barely had time to make the beds, put away the clothes folded on the chairs, and clear off the night table before she heard the fateful sound of the bell. What happened next proved that she'd been wise to take such precautions. The police, accompanied by the inevitable militiaman (luckily, not the same one as the first time), informed her courteously but firmly that they were looking for a certain Léa Lévy, six or seven years old. She had eluded a roundup about a year and a half earlier. Due to bureaucratic delays, her absence had not been noted before, but comparison between the Paris registration lists and those of the camp at Drancy confirmed that she had not been arrested along with her parents, who had been picked up in Bordeaux. Sister Saint-Germain listened to this story without showing much interest, explained that only about fifteen children were still boarding at the school, escorted the men to the sole dormitory still in use and only half full, let them count the occupied beds, and led the way to her office, where the mustached face of the old Maréchal beamed candidly down from a wall. She showed them her books, which were meticulously kept, ascribing Bénédicte's absence to a visit to her family after an illness. The child's papers were in order, and she could not be confused with Léa, as the girls were of different ages. The visitors halfheartedly opened a few doors, rummaged through some drawers, apologized, and left. When Sister Saint-Gabriel went to let the children out, she found them asleep, the younger child's head resting on the older one's lap.

In March of 1944, Léa received for her seventh birthday a game of jacks, a new jump rope, and an orange, which she shared with Bénédicte. Her report cards were maddeningly monotonous. Punctuality, ten out of ten. Attendance in church, ten. Neatness, orderliness, appearance, zero. Politeness, two. Conduct, zero. Industriousness in work, ten. Lessons, ten. Homework, ten. Sister Saint-Gabriel took the opportunity to deliver a short sermon to Léa, who put her own interpretation, however, on the fact that she had now reached the age of reason. Already insolent, she became argumentative. No matter what the nun said to persuade Léa to bring her behavior in line with her academic achievements, Léa found a riposte. Piety: "The chaplain says I'm very well behaved and that the good Lord must be pleased with me." Desire to emulate her friend, whose sweetness and discretion were admired by all: "Bénédicte is bored with everyone else. I'm the only one she likes, even if I am two years younger than she is." Gratitude: "My parents are very rich. I'll tell them to give you lots of money when they return. You'll be able to repaint the walls in the school and buy uniforms for little girls who don't have any money."

And that this return might come soon no longer seemed quite so impossible. After the German defeats on the Eastern front, undeniable despite the propaganda, came more and more insistent rumors of a future landing of Allied troops. In anticipation of that event, perhaps, the Resistance in Bordeaux gathered its meager forces together and brought off a few handsome acts of sabotage: nine locomotives blown up in Pessac, high-tension towers toppled near Arcachon, bridges and railways destroyed. At Saint-André-de-Cubzac, on Route 137, there was a real pitched battle that left one hundred and sixty-two Germans and only fourteen *résistants* dead. Sister Saint-Gabriel rushed to shut herself up in her office every evening with Sister Marthe. The two nuns removed their coifs, the better to listen to the Free French broadcast through the crackling static on their ancient crystal set.

Léa and Bénédicte were so excited that they couldn't even manage to read a book anymore. On June 6, Sister Saint-Gabriel took pity on them and let them sneak downstairs, unbeknownst to the other girls, to listen with her to the impassioned voice that announced the Normandy invasion before returning to the usual litany of incomprehensible sentences: "The pumpkin is in the pot," or "Philémon demands six bottles of Sauterne." Éric and Christian, who had joined the Free French Forces and been immediately promoted (one to general, the other to colonel), parachuted into Sainte-Mère-Église with their troops, seized enemy tanks, blew away all opposition to their victorious advance, and killed thousands of Germans, giving no quarter and taking no prisoners. They entered Paris right behind General Leclerc on August 25, 1944.

By that time, aside from Léa and Bénédicte, there had been no students left in the school since the end of June. The girls were thinner, with a feverish red tinge to their cheeks. Tormented by the heat and the waiting, they galloped restlessly along the hallways and staircases, unable to sit still for more than two minutes when the nuns tried to set them to peeling vegetables or sewing. They had caught scabies and were always scratching between their fingers. They had lost all appetite, just when the provisions brought by grateful families who'd come to get the other girls would have allowed them to eat a little better. Jam and butter had reappeared at snack time only to remain untouched. Léa alternated between periods of uncontrollable chattering, always on the subject of her parents' return, and long silences that were most unlike her.

In spite of the girls' pleading, Sister Saint-Gabriel refused to take them along on her brief errands outside the school. Not that she feared Léa's identity might be discovered: the Germans, collaborators, and militiamen now had much more to worry about than the arrest of a little Jewish girl, but for this very reason, there was such tension in the streets of Bordeaux, which the occupation forces had declared would be defended to the bitter end, that shooting was liable to break out over nothing at all. Soldiers were digging anti-tank trenches across the roadways. Troops were massing at the approach to the stone bridge, the only link to the right bank of the river. A blockhouse full of dynamite and munitions was blown up. In the harbor, explosions came from the scuttled ships as they slowly sank, one after the other.

Finally, late in August, the signal for departure was given. The people of Bordeaux peered through the slats of their closed shutters at the fleeing Germans. After the relatively orderly lines of the first trucks came a hodgepodge of different vehicles (mule carts, old requisitioned buses, cars sputtering along on bottles of cooking gas) packed with scruffy soldiers, their guns trained watchfully on the windows of the surrounding buildings. Another exodus had begun, toward the east this time. But the war raged on nearby, particularly in the pocket of Royan, which the enemy wanted to hold on to at all costs. German columns struck in reprisal, burning villages, hanging, shooting, disemboweling men, women, and children. Almost emptied of its occupiers but surrounded by danger, the city held its breath in the golden summer light. The last militiamen settled some scores before decamping. Small groups of men would suddenly appear in the deserted streets, shooting out shop windows with their revolvers, looting stores, tossing boxes and canned goods into a waiting car before speeding off.

The girls picked one of these oppressively sultry nights—which they spent jabbering away, for the most part, while they tossed and turned on their tangled sheets—to carry out a plan Bénédicte had at first opposed as too risky, then wearily accepted, and finally worked out through lengthy deliberation: they would leave the school to search for their parents. While exploring in daylight the underground shelter where they'd spent so many night-bombing raids, they'd noticed that the boards at the far end were half rotten, loose enough to be pried off with ease, revealing a tunnel that the girls were convinced would lead them to the street outside. In preparation for the momentous evening, they had filched Sister Saint-Gabriel's precious Wonder flashlight, which Léa had hidden beneath her mattress, and they'd even carefully greased the hinges of the door to the courtyard with a bit of lard.

So, that night they dressed in the dark and put their pillows lengthwise under their blankets, to make the beds look occupied in case of inspection. Léa carried the flashlight and Bénédicte wound their two jump ropes, knotted together, around her torso, as though she were a mountain climber. They went down the stone staircase, shadows among the other shadows lurking menacingly all around them. Opening the door without a sound, they paused on the threshold. The fragrant night seemed welcoming, and a light breeze caressed their bare legs, but the gardening sister's tool shed, where they would have to go first to get a pick and a shovel, seemed very far away. They tiptoed over to it in their sandals, however, crossing the pebbles quietly. Through the door they glimpsed a forest of bristling shapes where some man or animal might very well have been crouching. All of a sudden, outside the convent wall, they heard the sound of running, followed by an explosion. They looked at each other, then took to their heels in the same instant. Back in the dormitory, they couldn't help crying and sniffling with fear as they went back to bed.

At dawn the next morning, on August 28, two front-wheel-drive Citroëns with armed Resistance fighters lying across the mudguards cautiously entered the silent and tightly shuttered city. A stream of cars and trucks carrying shouting, ragged, bearded men flowed in behind them. In a twinkling, windows flew open, tricolor flags blossomed everywhere, and the streets filled with weeping, singing people who clambered onto the running boards of the vehicles to embrace the new arrivals. Church bells pealed. The city went mad: crowds poured into the buildings abandoned by the Germans, tossing furniture and papers out the window; cobblestones crashed through the windows of the Café Le Régent on the Place Gambetta; small, hesitant groups appeared on the Esplanade des Quinconces, then swelled to a throng that began to dance around while some young men climbed all the way to the top of the Colonne des Girondins.

At the school, Léa and Bénédicte were tearing all over the place like panicky wasps. At noon, someone came pounding on the outside gates. An impatient hand rang the bell until its jangling seemed to drill through the silence. Sister Saint-Gabriel hurried to open the door. Both girls ran after her, holding hands. When the gates were flung open, two forms appeared, black shapes in the blinding sunshine. Léa took a few steps forward. Bénédicte stood still. After their eyes had adjusted to the light, the girls saw a tall, raven-haired man wearing an officer's uniform and a tricolor armband standing on the cobblestones of the courtyard, alongside a young woman with big blue eyes, in jacket and trousers, with a forage cap tilted rakishly on her head. Bénédicte cried out, dropped her friend's hand, and flung herself into their arms. Léa retreated into the shadows and stuck her thumb in her mouth.

CHAPTER V

Despite this spectacular reappearance, Bénédicte's parents did not bear their daughter away in their triumphal chariot, her brow wreathed with laurels. Bordeaux had been liberated, but Germany wasn't beaten yet. Pushing the Boches back across the Rhine and going on to Berlin might take months. All this was explained at length to Bénédicte and Sister Saint-Gabriel in the nun's office. Besides, things were still too unsettled for them to allow their daughter to leave the school and stay with friends until the war was over. Vengeful collaborators or militiamen might yet prove quite dangerous, ready to fight on as long as possible. And anyway, it was only a few weeks before school would begin again. Bénédicte might as well stay there and start the year off right. But it was the nun who found the argument that won out over the child's tears and protests. Léa's parents had not yet returned, and she might not see them again for quite a while. What would happen to her without her friend?

Curious, Jean-Pierre and Jacqueline Gaillac asked about Léa. Lowering her voice as though the neighborhood were still crawling with spies listening at every door, Sister Saint-Gabriel told them about the child's arrival one night two years before, her Jewish origins, the roundup from which she had escaped, and the mystery surrounding her family's fate. Bénédicte's parents were silent, at first; they seemed saddened, and unable to look Sister Saint-Gabriel in the eye. Finally the father delivered a short speech that left the nun somewhat perplexed. The deportees—Jews, Resistance fighters, prisoners of war—were all currently in camps scattered more or less throughout Germany and Poland. One couldn't expect to see them again for months yet. The Russians and Western Allies would try to use pincer movements as they advanced to hasten the liberation of the camps, but such massive numbers of people had been displaced that it was going to take a tremendous amount of time to repatriate everyone. So when the Gaillacs paid their school fees, they discreetly offered to add a little money for this Léa to whom their daughter seemed quite attached. Sister Saint-Gabriel thanked them, but this conversation had disturbed her, and later on she was never able to remember it without a shudder.

Perched on her mother's knees and safely nestled in her arms, Bénédicte had heard everything as she rested her head on her mother's shoulder.

"Perhaps you really should look after your friend," her father said. "When we come back, we'll help her find her parents, if they still haven't returned. In the meantime, I think she needs you."

Bénédicte looked up. She tossed her black hair, frowned, and after a moment, jumped off her mother's lap.

"You're right," she admitted. "I didn't know about all that. I'll stay with Léa. Without me, she'd only get into trouble."

She said goodbye to her parents and left the nun's office with reddened eyes and an armful of presents: chocolate bars, silver-wrapped strips of a greenish gum you could chew for hours but shouldn't ever swallow or you'd choke to death, cans of corned beef, and butter—things that would finally justify the use of an "extras box." She immediately went looking for Léa to share these treasures with her, but the little girl had disappeared. She was found in the cupboard where she'd been hidden during the police search.

From that day on, Léa's behavior changed. All September long, when it was still quite warm, she stubbornly refused to go anywhere. Now that the danger was over, the nuns tried to take her for walks. They told her how lovely the park was, where you could picnic by a pond returned to its goldfish and swans, and they praised the cool air of the Landes, where Sister Marthe's family had a little house the two girls would have been welcome to visit during the weekends. The nuns described the tall trees, the sand and its carpet of pine needles, the sap flowing from gashes in the tree trunks into tiny pots attached to the bark, the heady perfume from this resin. They tried to tempt Léa by boasting of orchard peaches, frothy milk, jars of honey and jam. It was a waste of time. And everyone was so hungry, too, for Bordeaux was without trains, ships, any means of transportation, and there was little food, probably even less meat and bread than there had been the year before.

Toward the end of a torrid day, worn out by Bénédicte's pleading, Léa did give in one time and agreed to take a short evening stroll to the Garonne River, if they would be back within the hour. In the street, she dragged her feet and stared down at her dusty sandals with their straps that had been mended a hundred times. The area all around the railroad station was in ruins. She never once looked up. But on the Quai de Paludate, Léa abruptly let go of Bénédicte's hand. Walking ahead of her, with her back to the child, was a woman in a lightweight summer coat and straw hat, a dark, slim figure in the sunshine. Léa began to run. She caught up with the woman and grabbed her skirt. The lady turned around, smiled, and reached out to pat her head. Léa started violently away, like a frightened animal. After this scene, it was hopeless. She refused to leave the school, not even for an hour. She fell to the floor when they tried to dress her to go out. In the street, she would begin screaming.

So they gave up taking her for walks, and Bénédicte stayed inside as well, unwilling to leave Léa even for a single second. But the child was no longer the same. Docile and silent, aside from her tantrums about going outside, she wandered around the school like a wraith, sucking her thumb. Gone were the rages, the explosions, the bravado. Éric and Christian had returned to the realm of books, and despite Bénédicte's best efforts, were no longer brought to life by two little girls in pleated skirts. Léa picked at the meager fare set before her, simply shook her head at the rare treats she was offered, and dozed over old magazines from before the war. She slept a great deal. They would find her lying on her bed in the dormitory in the middle of the day, now that she'd been forbidden to go to her cupboard, which had been locked up for good.

She came to life only at the ringing of the doorbell. Wherever she was—awake or asleep, or later on, sitting in the classroom—her keen hearing would pick up the sound. No matter what time it was, the sister who went to open the door would see her appear out of nowhere at her side. Visitor after visitor would discover this disheveled little girl, in a skirt with a perpetually torn hem dangling down to her dusty shoes, standing out in the courtyard, rain or shine, staring at the strangers for a moment with her thumb in her mouth, sometimes coming closer to peer into their faces, as if her memory might be playing tricks on her, requiring this extra scrutiny. Then she would turn and walk away. Another girl, a bit older, would run up, look at her inquisitively, and trudge off with her friend.

The reopening of the school in October didn't change a thing. The students who expected to find a bragging wild child, so quick to taunt them and defend herself, scratching and biting anyone who dared come close, were dumbfounded by this mute little phantom who ignored all their teasing. Some girls even undid the belt of her smock or pulled her hair, after circling slowly around her to make sure she wasn't going to lash out on the attack. Others sidled up to her, shaking their fingers and chanting, "Nyah, nyah!" But she simply shrugged, so it wasn't fun to make sport of her anymore. Besides, loyal Bénédicte was constantly on guard, and the rest of the girls respected her after hearing so much at home about her parents' heroic feats in the Resistance.

Bénédicte's mother and father sent her packages and letters but never mentioned the fate of the deportees. The nuns were quite worried about Léa, whose apathy they found even harder to bear than her former unruliness. When Sister Marthe checked the dormitories late at night, making sure that everything was in order, she often stopped at the child's bedside and watched her toss uneasily in her sleep. Unlike Sister Saint-Gabriel, who had no family, Sister Marthe had nieces and nephews. One night, she realized that for two years, no one had kissed Léa or given her a hug. She hesitated; then, gathering together the folds of her skirt and holding her rosary so as not to make any noise, she carefully bent down and lightly kissed Léa's forehead. Without awakening, the little girl began to make tiny sucking movements with her lips, like an infant wanting to nurse. Standing up straight again, the nun looked quickly around the room, as though she'd done something wrong. If any student had seen her, she'd have been accused of favoritism, and Léa would have been labeled a teacher's pet. But this didn't stop Sister Marthe from doing the same thing on subsequent nights, always with the utmost precaution.

Sister Saint-Gabriel tried to find out when prisoners would be returning from the camps but was told that they were only trickling back as yet and that there was almost no information about them. She went to the prefecture, which was still in a state of confusion despite the arrival in September of General Chaban-Delmas to help restore order and prepare for a visit from General de Gaulle himself. Officials there were overwhelmed by all sorts of administrative problems (the difficulties of weeding out collaborators, of provisioning the city, where supplies were so low that there had been strikes and street demonstrations)—and hadn't time to pay attention to the fate of one little girl, and a Jewish one at that. Sister Saint-Gabriel was advised to hand Léa over to the child welfare authorities until the return of her parents, who had left, according to their records, for an unspecified destination. Sister Saint-Gabriel could not bring herself to do this.

One April day in 1945, after managing to wangle some precious offal out of the butcher for an astronomical price, Sister Saint-Gabriel undid the newspaper wrapping to display her prize to the sister in charge of the kitchen. A horrible photograph appeared, showing piles of naked, skeletal corpses. She smoothed it out with the flat of her hand and read a few lines presented as the testimony of a "survivor": "Thousands perished. At Auschwitz, thousands were gassed and burned. Those murderers! My mother, my wife, my child—

they killed them all. I heard them screaming in the gas chamber, one last scream let out by two thousand people in a single voice!" Staggered, Sister Saint-Gabriel crumpled the newspaper into a ball and flung it into the oven. Then she pulled herself together. It had to be an exaggeration, some story cooked up by a journalist. And anyway, it was a Communist paper. Nothing she'd heard at police headquarters had suggested that the prisoners of this war could have been treated like that. They had supposedly been weakened by hard labor, had lost weight because of privation (like most of the French population, actually, if it came to that), and some were ill, from tuberculosis or even typhus, because of the poor sanitary conditions—but no one had said anything about mass murder.

About ten days later, however, she came across another article, this time in a more trustworthy newspaper, *Le Figaro*. What struck her was not so much the article itself as the few awkward and confused lines of introduction written by the editor.

"I hesitated before offering our readers this haunting account that James de Coquet has just sent to us, a piece written with that concern for the truth that has always distinguished his work and made it so noteworthy. I am not unaware of the anguish and revulsion that may be inspired by the description of sights like these. But I believe that it is our duty to present these facts, to put them on record, to offer the clearest possible picture, and to do so at a time when the imminence of victory is preparing a world exhausted by horror for the balm of oblivion."

What she read there chilled her heart. On her way back to her office, she crossed the courtyard. The chestnut trees were in flower, and beneath their branches recess was in full swing. While the older girls kicked a ball around, the younger ones were busy with jump ropes, hopscotch, and noisy games of tag. Off in a quiet corner, Bénédicte was playing alone at handball, her skirt flouncing merrily as she chanted in her clear voice, "One hand, now the other, one foot, now the other, lil' crossover, big crossover, turnabout . . ." Not far from her, Léa was huddled listlessly on a bench, sucking her thumb. Sister Saint-Gabriel gazed at her, appalled. Things couldn't go on like this. The child was losing her mind. And she herself would soon break down beneath the weight of her own responsibility.

That evening she went to get Léa, whom she found in the study hall where the students did their homework under the supervision of a novice. Sister Saint-Gabriel spotted Léa immediately, as hers was the only face missing from the row of heads politely raised at the nun's approach. Leaning on one forearm, the little girl was doodling distractedly with her pen on some scrap paper, enlarging a big smear of violet ink with decorative flourishes. She hadn't even noticed the visitor, who took her hand and led her quietly away. In her office, Sister Saint-Gabriel told Léa bluntly that she was going to take her to Paris, where all the deportees were being sent. It was useless to wait for her parents to come looking for her in Bordeaux. Why not save them the trouble?

Léa perked up in a twinkling, like a wilted azalea soaking up a bucket of water, its petals turning pink and smooth again. The color returned to her cheeks, and she instantly recovered the power of speech.

"What about Bénédicte?" she asked. "Is she coming with us?"

"No, that's impossible. I haven't the right to let her leave the school without permission from her parents. And the trains are completely packed, you know. They weren't able to get them running again until just a short while ago. I don't even know how I'm going to manage getting tickets for the two of us."

Léa seemed downcast for a moment.

"It doesn't matter," she said finally. "I'm eight now, I'm grown up. And I'll tell Mama and Papa to invite her right away to come stay with us on the Boulevard des Invalides. You'll let her come, won't you?"

The nun was about to reply that they were right in the middle of the school year, but quickly agreed when she saw how eager the child was. Léa dashed off to tell Bénédicte the news. Her arrogance and unruliness had returned in a flash. She burst into the study hall and rushed over to her friend's desk.

"I'm leaving for Paris!" she shouted. "I'm going to take the train with Sister Saint-Gabriel to go find my parents. I'm never coming back here, ever, but you, you can come see me immediately, as soon as they've arrived home, all right?" Turning toward the rest of the class, who stared at her in astonishment, pens frozen in mid-stroke, she yelled, "My papa's going to send the chauffeur in the big car for Bénédicte. But the bunch of you won't be seeing me again any time soon!"

As it turned out, it was several days before they were able to get on a train. Every morning Sister Saint-Gabriel arrived at the Gare Saint-Jean at dawn: in one hand she carried her old black briefcase (containing a change of underwear for herself and the child, and a snack wrapped in greaseproof paper), and with the other she held on to Léa, who was dancing with excitement and never stopped prattling shrilly about everything she would soon be seeing again in Paris. It was as though she had recovered her memory all at once and wished to forestall any future lapses by taking inventory of her possessions.

"And my papa will let me sit next to him in the car, and it'll be my mama who takes me to school and you know we don't have uniforms there, Sister, we can wear whatever we like, I've seen the girls getting out of school lots of times when I was out for a walk with my nanny, and I'll make a pretty necklace for Bénédicte from my box of beads, and I'll let her play with my hoop, and I'll ask the sewing lady who makes my mama's dresses to sew new clothes for all my dolls, they must have been so bored without me, poor things, and I'll make sure nothing got broken in my tea set, and Zélie, that's the cook, she'll make me some cocoa to pour into the cups, they're china with pink flowers and a gold rim, and you know, the handles are very very fragile, Sister, and I'll tell Bénédicte to be extra careful with the one that was mended, when she comes to play with me, and I'd forgotten my big red car, it has pedals and a horn, I'm allowed to play with it in the hall—you know, the hall is very long, Sister—but only if I don't make a mess, and it's true that one day I broke the big blue vase standing on the floor next to the door but I won't do it again and besides my nanny fixed it."

Sister Saint-Gabriel had quickly noticed, listening to this litany, that Léa appeared to have forgotten how many years had gone by. The little girl who hated to be treated like a baby by her schoolmates didn't seem to realize that she would be too big to fit inside her pedal-car, that her dolls would no longer interest her, and that Bénédicte, if she ever did visit her one day, would have no desire, at ten years old, to play tea party. Sister Saint-Gabriel kept her thoughts to herself, however, and soon, overwhelmed by the child's babbling, she stopped paying any attention to it. Besides, that piercing voice was delivering this monologue against a deafening background of noise in the station, a racket of screeching axles, whistles, jets of steam, the banging of luggage carts, and the shouts of those who had managed to clamber onto the train and were calling desperately out the windows to their families, who dragged their suitcases down the platform as fast as they could. People cursed, pushed, trampled their neighbors' feet, even punched one another.

It was only on the third day, after returning twice to the school after dark—Sister Saint-Gabriel haggard and mute with fatigue, preceded by a capering Léa, still chirping away—that the stationmaster arranged for them to get on a night train. He made room for the nun in a crowded compartment and wound up settling the child in the baggage rack, on a coat meant to keep the wooden bars from digging into her ribs, with the black briefcase for a pillow. The journey was interminable, interrupted by long stops in the middle of nowhere, with sudden jolting departures that drew moans from the human magma jammed into the broken-down seats. From the baggage rack came the constant sibilant hum of Léa's voice, continuing its whispered soliloquy. Léa was the first passenger to sit up at sunrise, which found them still far from the capital.

The same chaos reigned in the Gare d'Austerlitz. Sister Saint-Gabriel had never been to Paris. She finally managed to catch the attention of another traveler, a woman who pulled a blunt pencil and a crumpled scrap of paper from her purse to show the nun how to reach her destination on the Métro. After making many mistakes, they reached the Saint-François-Xavier station, where the good sister was cheered by the discovery of a church when they emerged onto the boulevard. Confused, exhausted, she summoned a last burst of authority to drag Léa inside, where, after a hasty genuflection and sign of the cross, she collapsed onto a chair. A few moments later, she saw a priest come in, passing his stole around his neck as he prepared to enter the confessional. Sister Saint-Gabriel went over and spoke with him in a low voice while the little girl, at whom the two adults glanced uneasily now and then, climbed around on the benches, holding her arms straight out at her sides and buzzing like an airplane.

Thanks to the priest's directions, they soon found the address they were looking for, which was quite close by. Just as the nun was about to push open the wrought-iron door of the handsome building, the balconies of which overlooked the wide, tree-lined boulevard, Léa's excitement drained away. She took a step backward.

"This isn't it," she said.

Sister Saint-Gabriel leaned back to check the number again, squinting in the spring sunlight reflecting off the tall windows.

"But we're at number 27. That's the address you've always given me and the one that's on your papers, too."

"This isn't it," repeated Léa, on the verge of tears.

Repressing a shrug, the exasperated nun rang the bell. The door clicked open after a few seconds, and a voice from inside the concierge's lodge called out, "What is it?"

Gazing intently at the elevator door, which was decorated in bas-relief with a kind of copper medallion showing the bust of a woman holding a child in her arms, Léa turned so white that the nun grabbed her arm, fearing she was about to faint.

Broom in hand, the concierge appeared, a sturdy woman in an apron with her gray hair pulled back in a bun.

"Monsieur and Madame Lévy, please," said the nun.

"Who?"

"Monsieur and Madame Lévy. I'm returning their daughter Léa to them. They do live here, don't they?"

"They haven't lived here for at least three years," replied the concierge, gaping in astonishment at the skinny little girl who was staring fixedly at her. "They left a long time ago, at the end of '41, beginning of '42, I think. They continued paying their rent for a few months after that, and then, nothing. The owner finally rented the apartment to someone else."

"But their clothing? Their furniture?"

"You know, Sister, I have no idea where you've been, but here we had the Occupation, the war. There was a lot of coming and going upstairs—the militia, the police . . . And then, with those people, you're never really sure what's going on, where the money comes from, what belongs to whom. They had money, the Lévys, I'll grant you that—you should have seen the furs that woman had, her husband's cars . . . But what with the family, friends, there was a whole swarm of . . . well, Israelites . . . parading in and out of there after they left, especially during the roundups in July. With the owner's permission, we finally changed the lock. He's the one who took care of clearing out the apartment, but there wasn't much left, according to what he told me."

"Do you have his address?"

"He's dead. The building was taken over by a company. I'll be glad to give you the name, but it won't really get you anywhere."

During this conversation, the two women had forgotten about Léa. Apparently fascinated by the concierge's apartment, the child slipped through the door unnoticed. Screams then erupted, followed by the sound of fighting. The women dashed inside. A little girl in a checked smock was sitting at a big table covered in oilcloth.

"It's mine!" shrieked Léa, trying to wrest from the other girl a huge box of multicolored beads sorted into various compartments. "Give it back to me! It's mine!"

Terrified, the other girl let go. Sister Saint-Gabriel made as if to intervene, but the concierge glanced over at her Henri II sideboard, graced with a ravishing silver coffee service on a tray, complete with coffeepot, milk jug, sugar bowl and tongs, as well as cups and saucers, plus a silver samovar that added an exotic touch completely out of keeping with the rest of the décor, which was decidedly modest. Completely absorbed in her quarrel, Léa had not noticed any of these things.

"Yvette," said the concierge, "charity begins at home. This little girl is poor, she hasn't any toys. Give her that box, and I'll buy you another."

Yvette wanted to protest, but an icy look from her mother made it clear that this was not the time. The concierge hurried to close the box, wrap it up in newspaper and string, and hand the package to Léa, who clasped it to her heart.

"Well, Sister, goodbye," said the woman, taking the nun by the shoulders to direct her back out to the street. "The only advice I can give you is to go to city hall. You'll probably find out something there. Or else, hold on, why don't you just pop over to the Hôtel Lutétia, on the Boulevard Raspail? A luxury hotel, where they're sending all the repatriated people. They get everything they could possibly want, it seems. They're stuffed with meat, foie gras, and fine wines, while the rest of us, the real French, we're dying of hunger, as usual. But you know, your couple, they're probably in America—I'm told that's where quite a lot of their kind went when the war began. They'll come get their daughter, eventually. I wish you good luck, in any case."

And the heavy glass door closed behind Sister Saint-Gabriel and Léa.

CHAPTER VI

The Hôtel Lutétia wasn't far, according to a woman passing by; they could easily walk there. On the way they passed the Lycée Victor-Duruy. The trees in the school garden showed off their spring foliage over the surrounding wall. White flowers rained down from the tall chestnuts, their branches stirred by the occasional breeze. School was letting out, and students were pouring from the gate, flocking together in chattering groups. When they caught sight of their mothers, the girls would run off to join them, swinging their book satchels, their hair flying in the wind, dappled by sunshine and shade. The young women in their tight-waisted suits and hats with little veils would hasten forward, dainty purses waltzing in the crooks of their arms, stocking seams painted perfectly straight on the backs of their carefully stained calves. They leaned down to kiss their daughters, tenderly straightening a collar, tightening up a loose braid, flicking away a shred of tree bark, taking the heavy satchels from their hands as the girls turned around one last time to wave endless goodbyes to their classmates, as if they would never see them again. Still wearing the same worn and faded navy blue skirt that had long ago lost any trace of a pleat, her frizzy hair haphazardly pinned back by two big barrettes, Léa walked by the girls without giving them a single glance. She was too busy clutching the enormous box, which kept slipping in her grasp, and she paid no more attention to the school children than she had to the revelations of the concierge.

"My feet hurt," she grumbled after a few minutes' walk. "Is it still far away, where we're going?"

"I don't think so," replied her companion, who was afraid of getting lost and stopped at every intersection to rummage through her big black briefcase, put on her glasses, and look up at the street signs.

"What kind of hotel is it?"

"A very fancy one, it seems."

"Ah," said Léa, quickening a pace that had begun to flag. "Then my parents might be there. If that horrible concierge wouldn't let them into their apartment, they must've had to find someplace to put their things before coming to get me in Bordeaux. They really like luxury hotels. Papa took me to the Plaza one day," she added after a moment, as though struck by a distant recollection. "He picked me up and sat me down on the bar to introduce me to the bartender. He even let me have a sip of his cocktail," she added excitedly. "I remember Mama scolded him when we got home."

She fell silent and seemed lost in her memories for the rest of their walk.

After going up the Rue de Sèvres and turning onto the Boulevard Raspail, as she'd been told to do, Sister Saint-Gabriel soon realized she'd found the right place when she spotted the people massed before the hotel. It was a strange group, she saw as she drew closer: mostly old men and women, some of whom had babies in their arms. The crowd was listless, apathetic. Children slept curled up right there on the sidewalk. Almost all the adults were thin and shabbily dressed, and they held signs on which names were scrawled in big, uneven letters, next to tiny identification photos that were indecipherable from half a yard away. It was clear from their rumpled clothes and tired faces, from the way they let their clumsy, handmade signs droop toward the ground, that they had been waiting for a long while and had come there many times before. Some were all hunched over, their hands buried in their pockets, as though they felt cold despite the delightfully warm air. With Léa in tow, Sister Saint-Gabriel joined the throng. When she tried to question her neighbors, she encountered only silence and indifference.

The crowd came abruptly to life when two buses with red crosses on their sides and roofs pulled up in front of the hotel. People held their signs straight, craned their necks, closed ranks, murmured to one another. Children awoke, rubbed their eyes, scrambled to their feet. Finally, the rear doors opened. Stretcher bearers hurried into the hotel, as though trying through such haste to protect their charges from prying eyes. And yet there didn't seem to be anything beneath the brown blankets draped across their stretchers. All whispering died away. Then about fifty men in striped pajamas appeared, deathly pale, gaunt, wearing caps that could not conceal their shaven skulls. They crossed the sidewalk with infinite slowness, shielding their eyes with their hands as if to ward off the radiant sunshine. The crowd, which had parted to let the stretchers through, now shuddered violently and hurled itself forward like a wave, shrieking, calling to the newcomers, screaming out harshly resonant names that sounded like stones tumbling against one another in the rising tide. The new arrivals shrank back. A woman in a threadbare coat, too warm for the season, fell at the feet of one shuffling man, threw an arm around his knees, and with her other hand forced the little girl with her to shove a roneograph photo under her captive's nose.

"Adam Zylberstein!" she wailed in a strong foreign accent. "He's tall, a big man, with curly brown hair. He delivered bolts of cloth for a wholesale clothing manufacturer. He was picked up in Belleville, in June of '42. Do you know him, monsieur? Have you seen him anywhere?"

Thrown off balance by her attack, the man had caught hold of a comrade's shoulder to keep from falling. He freed himself with a convulsive movement of his whole body, a true gesture of repulsion, and walked on, without even looking at the leaflet the child was waving in front of his face. The woman collapsed on the sidewalk and just sat there, her arms hanging limply. Taking advantage of the dejection that had settled once more over the crowd for a moment, Sister Saint-Gabriel cut ahead of the entire line, dragging Léa along by the collar of her blouse as the child gripped her box tightly in both hands. They managed to slip through the hotel door barely an instant before it closed. As Sister Saint-Gabriel was gagging on the odor of disinfectant that immediately stung their nostrils, she received a cloud of DDT sprayed directly in her face by a uniformed nurse stationed just inside the door. Blinded by tears, half-strangled by coughing, she wiped herself off with a fold of her skirt. It was some time before she could see again.

In that huge lobby, the only things that corresponded to Sister Saint-Gabriel's idea of a deluxe hotel were the walls covered with gilt moldings and the ceiling with its tinkling chandelier. This vast space had been divided into small cubicles, each one furnished with two chairs and a wooden table at which sat people of various ages, in civilian clothes, interviewing the visitors. The partitions separating these improvised offices were completely covered with photos like those being brandished by the throng outside. Dozens, hundreds, thousands of names and faces seemed to jump out at the nun: men in suits and ties gazing solemnly into the camera, smiling women with babies on their laps, boys in their best clothes, little girls wearing starched dresses and big bows in their hair. There was even an entire class lined up on benches, sitting with their hands quietly folded, grouped around their teacher. The captions overlapped one another, as if in a desperate hurry to speak. "Have you seen, encountered, heard about . . . Can you give me any news, good or bad, regarding . . . my parents, my husband, my wife, my son, my daughter . . . picked up in Paris, Bordeaux, Marseille . . . in '42, '43, '44 . . . last seen in Drancy, Pithiviers, Beaune-la-Rolande . . . left on convoy number 10, 25, 58 . . . for Buchenwald, Ravensbrück, Auschwitz . . . Sincere thanks, large reward, eternally grateful . . ." Had half the French population disappeared, then—leaving behind only these faint traces, these fading pictures and names so full of consonants—while the other half was trying frantically to find them? Sister Saint-Gabriel was well aware that people had been shot, imprisoned, deported, but was it possible that *thousands*, and perhaps more, had been torn from their everyday lives?

She was reassured by a solitary poster tacked up on a nearby panel. It showed, from the back, two men helping a third man: they were all in striped pajamas and all walking, beneath a blue sky, toward a typically French church steeple glinting in the morning sunshine. "Political prisoners, deportees, labor conscripts," said the text. "If you have witnessed an act of cruelty during your detention, or any action contrary to the rules of war as laid down by the Geneva Convention, report it to your local police station. The guilty will be punished." So there were still laws, policemen to enforce them, victims and criminals. One had only to appeal to the responsible authorities, and order would eventually be restored. Sister Saint-Gabriel turned toward a little cubicle, one with an empty chair, but in doing so she noticed, lined up along a wall, the stretchers that had been unloaded from the bus outside only moments before. She had thought they were empty, and she had been wrong. A skull with black eye sockets, bony temples, protruding teeth, and cheeks devoured by stubble had just risen up, all by itself. The nun reached out instinctively to shield Léa from the sight, but the child simply pushed her hand away impatiently.

"Sister, what are we doing here? Let's go! I want to show my beads to Bénédicte."

"What are you talking about, Léa? You know perfectly well we're here to find your parents."

"But they're not here!"

"How can you be so sure of that?"

Putting her precious box down on the floor, setting it on edge between her calves to make sure she wouldn't lose it, Léa pointed all around her at the immense room: skulls sitting on their stretchers, cut off cleanly at the neck by brown blankets lying flat on the canvas; groups of detainees in striped pajamas, staggering, drunk with exhaustion; a nurse tending to a skeletal woman in a black dress three times too big for her, collapsed on a chair like a sack of bones; famished-looking visitors jostling one another in front of the bulletin boards, craning their necks to inspect every scrap of information; the sick, pale and drawn, returning from their X-ray examinations with envelopes tucked beneath their arms; doctors in white coats making their way through the crowd, their stethoscopes bouncing gently on their chests. And the nun was suddenly struck by the fact that despite the great press of people and activity, all this was going on in remarkable silence.

Léa gave a quick, silvery laugh, drawing a look of surprise from the elderly lady in a navy blue suit sitting at a table covered with papers in a nearby cubicle, the one with the empty chair.

"Why do you think my parents might be here?" asked Léa. "If they were back, they'd certainly have gone to get me before coming here to help all these poor people."

Sister Saint-Gabriel simply stared at her.

"But, well, Léa," she said finally, choosing her words with care, "don't you think they might themselves be among these unfortunate souls?"

This time the child burst out laughing.

"Oh, Sister, it's obvious you don't know my parents! They don't look anything at all like these people. You never believe me when I tell you that my father is very handsome, very elegant, and that my mother . . . Well, my mother would never, ever wear a dress like the one that woman over there has on."

And Léa pointed with a little wince of disgust at the shapeless black bag enveloping the pile of bones slumped on a chair.

"You always suspect me of boasting when I talk about them. I know that, but you'll see when they come back, you'll see."

So saying, she picked up her box and clutched it to her chest, pursing her lips like someone who has given up trying to get an absolute dummy to admit something that's as plain as day. Sister Saint-Gabriel shrugged and put her hand on the back of the child's neck to guide her over to the cubicle with the empty chair.

The elderly woman listened to the nun's story of the Lévys

and their daughter without interrupting, as though she already knew it by heart, merely jotting a few things down in a notebook. When the nun had finished, the woman handed her a form.

"If you would just fill this out, Sister, and give us the child's identification papers, we'll be able to place her in an institution. She doesn't remember the existence of other members of her family, you say? Still, who knows whether an aunt or uncle or cousin might not turn up one day after all. Thank you, in any case, for everything you've done for her."

"But we can easily keep her in our school until her parents arrive," replied Sister Saint-Gabriel. "I only came here to try to find them more quickly and to leave you our address, so that they'll know where to find her when they do return."

The old lady sighed.

"Léa," she said, without looking up at the child, "why don't you take a little walk around the hotel? You'll find some very lovely furniture to look at. And you must be hungry, too. So just go into the dining room, over there. They'll give you something to eat. We have a few administrative problems to settle, this nun and I. If you stayed with us, you'd be bored. Come back in about fifteen minutes."

Léa, who was indeed bored, did not need to be asked twice. As soon as she had trotted off, the old lady looked up again.

"Sister," she said, "I don't think you've fully grasped the scope of the catastrophe. If the parents of this child were Jews, if they were deported to Auschwitz, on the dates you've given me—during 1942, in other words—then there is every reason to believe they will not be coming back."

"Do you think they're being held in Russia? I've heard rumors about that . . ."

"I think they're dead."

"But they were . . . I mean, they're young, healthy, there's no reason why they wouldn't have survived conditions in the camps, even if they were hard, as they claim. I've heard that several thousand Jews were deported. Really, they can't all be dead."

"As far as we know, almost eighty thousand left: men, women, and children. As of now, a few more than two thousand have returned. If the survivors' stories are to be believed, there is little chance of us seeing many more come back."

Aghast, the nun collapsed against the back of her chair, mopping her brow.

"So just fill out these forms, Sister," continued the woman, "even if you do intend to keep looking after the child. She'll be needing these papers, if only to obtain her parents' death certificate. I'll leave you to it. I'll be back for them in a few minutes."

In the meantime, still lugging around her box of beads, Léa was looking for a place where she could comfortably eat the chocolate bar and piece of bread she'd been given in the dining room. There she'd seen trays being prepared, loaded with appetizing dishes, nicely presented, and bottles of wine with old labels. This led her to think she might have been mistaken about the quality of the hotel and that if she followed one of the Lutétia's liveried staff up the imposing red-carpeted staircase she saw before her, she would find people who were different from that wretched humanity swarming in the lobby. And what she saw upstairs seemed to bear this out.

The landing gave onto a long corridor that turned several times at right angles. Big pearl-gray doors framed with moldings in a darker shade lined the walls. The man in livery pushed open one of the doors, and Léa had just enough time to notice a large, richly furnished room, although she couldn't manage to catch a glimpse of its occupant. She began by visiting the rest rooms, where the marble sinks and gilded faucets made an excellent impression on her. Yes, her parents might very well have chosen this hotel as a place where they would stay and rest after their long trip, before taking the train again for Bordeaux. Perhaps her father was here, busy tying his tie in front of the mirror, while her mother was powdering her nose, sitting on a little mahogany chair that matched the dressing table, like the ones she'd just seen a moment ago. An image—like those fleeting, incomplete scenes that would visit her briefly in the evening, in the dormitory, before vanishing as though swept away by the wind—now suddenly appeared to her, tenacious and precise. Her father was wearing a light gray suit; a fancy handkerchief of white silk gleamed in his breast pocket. From a case covered in black faille and bearing his initials inlaid with gold he withdrew a pastel-colored, gold-tipped cigarette. Her mother, a delicate brunette in a dress of sea-green muslin sprinkled with pearls, the dusky wing of her hair caressing her cheek, was bringing a tube of lipstick to her mouth with a rapt expression that Léa, standing next to her, had often imitated to amuse herself. The long necklace her mother wore looped twice around her neck clinked on the marble top of the dressing table. Next to the face-powder box, a bottle of champagne sat enthroned in an ice bucket with a white napkin wrapped around its neck.

Her heart pounding, Léa knocked on the door of the room where the hotel employee had left his tray. When there was no answer, she summoned up her courage and went in. In that sumptuous room, a skeletal man with a bald skull was stretched out on the immaculate sheets, his bony and deformed hands lying palms up, the fingers slightly curled. The pink satin bolster of his immense bed made the sagging skin of his face seem even yellower. He hadn't bothered to look up when Léa came in. The tray was sitting on a table, untouched. The silver dish covers the child had seen placed over that mouth-watering food downstairs hadn't even been removed. Suddenly afraid, Léa turned around, tiptoed out, and closed the door quietly behind her.

In all the rooms into which she peeked, after receiving no response to the polite little knock she made with one knuckle, Léa saw the same thing: men, women, alone or in couples, lying on their beds, silent, eyes closed, like wax mannequins stripped of their wigs and laid out in the showroom of a large furniture store before being piled into a truck and sent off to a factory to be melted down and refashioned according to the specifications of the next client. She'd read that about mannequins in the feature pages of a children's magazine. Léa had never seen any dead people, aside from the mangled and bloody bodies glimpsed at a distance after the bombing raids on Bordeaux. This was how she imagined people looked when they'd died of illness or old age. But why would anyone have turned one of the loveliest hotels in Paris into a morgue? Was it customary to bring people to a luxury hotel after they were dead, so that they could have at least one chance to enjoy the pleasures of life, if they'd never tasted them when they were alive?

Confused and upset, Léa decided to stop looking around for the moment and to continue her search in another part of the hotel. She had just happened upon an empty room and thought it would be a good place in which to eat her snack at last and open her box of beads, which she was eager to examine. Like the other rooms, this one was large and magnificently furnished. Léa didn't dare sit on the spread of quilted satin brocade hanging in perfect folds over the turned wooden feet of the bed, so she plopped down instead on the thick carpet, with her back against one of the sides of a big polished bombé chest of drawers with pulls in the shape of elaborately worked rings of gilt metal. She unwrapped her chocolate bar, stuck it into her piece of bread, and set the whole thing down on a scrap torn from the newspaper tied around her box of beads, so as not to leave any crumbs. Then she turned on a porcelain lamp with a rose-colored shade of pleated material, undid the package, and opened the box to admire her beads. There were all kinds of them, carefully sorted into compartments: large, small, round, square, oval, white, red, green—enough to make all different kinds of necklaces and bracelets with the cords provided in the set. Absorbed in the contemplation of her treasure, she reached out for her bread and chocolate. Her fingers touched another hand.

Léa started and looked up. A corpse had appeared out of nowhere and was watching her. It was the same skull as the severed heads sitting on the stretchers downstairs: ashen skin mottled with red blotches and stretched over slanting cheekbones so sharp they seemed about to slice through it; big dark circles under the eyes; yellow teeth protruding from receding gums; chapped white lips. No hair, no eyebrows, no eyelashes. No beard, either, but that wasn't surprising since the corpse, judging from its height, and if one could imagine estimating its age, was that of a boy who couldn't have been more than thirteen or fourteen years old. Léa tried to run away, but the icy hand held tight to her wrist. This exaggeratedly large hand was at the end of a knobby stick partly covered by the floppy sleeve of a gray-and-white striped pajama top just like the ones worn by the men who had gotten off the bus a little earlier. The boy was on all fours. He had probably crawled out of the space between the opposite side of the chest and the wall, where he'd been crouching in this room so neat and clean that it had seemed completely unoccupied.

He sat back on his heels and studied Léa. In the frozen face of that living corpse, the nocturnal eyes, which seemed to be all pupil, burned with a dull flame whose black light turned inward, as though a vision of hell had seared and reversed the lens, leaving only the inner surface intact and capable of sight. The corpse raised the hand holding the bread and chocolate to its mouth; the teeth in their bleeding gums began to nibble delicately, and with care. Releasing Léa's wrist, the other hand rose jerkily into the air, and a finger touched her cheek, its claw-like nail sinking into the plump rosy flesh, where it left a crescent-shaped mark. Then the hand grabbed a lock of her hair and tugged on it, as if testing its strength. Léa began quietly to cry. The finger wiped off a tear and brought it to the tongue, which licked it up. The eyes, so blind and yet so wise, grew even bigger, as though preparing to engulf the little girl in some deep well of viscous truth. Finally they looked down at the box of beads. The claw began to poke around in them. It scattered them, gathered them together, sent them rolling into one another. It picked up a handful, let them dribble back into the box, did this again, and again, ten times, more and more lazily. And all at once, as if he'd received an electric shock, the boy sat up, dropped the bread and chocolate, grabbed the box, and turned it upside down over Léa's head. The child sat stunned, at first, by the extent of the disaster. The beads had fallen all over the carpet. There was a small pile in a fold of her skirt, and she could feel the cool surface of a few inside the neckline of her blouse, while others were caught in her hair.

"I didn't mean to make you angry," she finally wailed in despair, as a rainbow-colored shower tumbled down with a tinkling noise onto the tiny glass beads piled up in her lap. "I only came in here because I'm looking for my parents. I thought they might be in one of these rooms. You see, they went away on a trip three years ago, and they haven't come back yet."

The boy had collapsed onto his heels, apparently exhausted by his fit. There was no change in his expressionless face, but the hand that had fallen back onto the striped material slowly rose again to trace a graceful spiral in the air, an arabesque uncoiling toward the window like a curl of smoke. The mouth pursed up as though in preparation for a grotesque kiss.

"Poof," it said.

The child looked at him without understanding, and searching frantically for something to say, whispered, "My name is Léa."

A rictus twisted the cracked lips, to which a few bread crumbs still clung, and from the withered throat, thrust forward by an enormous Adam's apple that stuck out like the barrel of a gun, another sound emerged: cackling laughter, followed by the phlegmy cough of a chain-smoker. The hand raised a striped sleeve to show, tattooed on skin that seemed glued to the bone, a series of blue numbers. Then the face became impassive once again.

Léa was silent, but something in his eyes drew her on, and

she could feel a question rising from deep down inside her, rising inexorably to her mouth in spite of all her efforts to repress it, rising up until suddenly she blurted out breathlessly, "My parents—you know, right? You know where they are, don't you!"

The rictus reappeared, wider and wider, but must have proved too painful for the wounded lips and gums, because it quickly vanished. The boy leaned forward, and with the precision of an entomologist searching for rare insects in tall grass, he picked out the beads still caught in Léa's curls, one by one. Then he lifted up a lock of her hair, came so close that she could feel his feverish breath, and murmured rapidly in her ear.

"Gassed. Poisoned like rats. Burned in an oven. Turned into black smoke. Poof, your parents. Poof."

Léa reared back, shoved aside the arm still holding her hair, jumped up, and ran from the room with a strangled cry.

PART TWO

CHAPTER VII

"That child is ungrateful, if you want my frank opinion."

The visitor brushed a crumb from her gray "New Look" skirt, with its long hem falling gracefully over her crossed legs, and buried her sharp nose in her teacup. Her lipstick left a purplish mark on the china. She dabbed at her mouth with an embroidered napkin, taking care not to smudge the corners of her lips. Her bleached bangs frizzled over mean little eyes she had tried to make larger by loading mascara onto thick strips of false eyelashes.

"Not at all," said Jacqueline Gaillac. "Bringing her your daughters' outgrown clothes was very kind of you, and I thank you for your thoughtfulness. It's just that Léa is a bit sensitive. She must have been afraid that later on, in school, the other students would notice that her dresses were hand-me-downs, and would feel sorry for her. She only accepts things from Bénédicte. Those two are constantly exchanging outfits."

"All the same, there's a difference between that and handing the package back to me without even opening it, saying thank you but she doesn't have the same taste in clothes as my girls, and then curtsying in a way that I just couldn't help feeling was sarcastic."

"Oh, Léa always curtsies in front of grownups. She never lost the habit, even though Bénédicte teases her, saying sixteen is a little old for that sort of thing. She's very well brought up, you know."

"I don't doubt it, since she has you to thank for her education. It was so brave, Madame Gaillac, so generous of you to take in that child. When I think that no one even knows where she comes from!"

"Léa lost her parents during the war. In spite of all our efforts we were never able to find a trace of her family, if she has any left. Her father and mother had retained their Russian nationality. Their marriage certificate indicates that her maternal grandparents had remained in Russia. Given the current political situation, now is not the time to go looking for information over there. In any case, we did try, in 1946, through our embassy, but of course we got nowhere. There were so many displaced persons during that terrible time. And then her grandparents were already elderly. They must be dead, by now."

The visitor lifted her eyes to heaven and sighed. When she took her leave, Jacqueline Gaillac watched her go with a pleasure she barely concealed behind polite expressions of regret. "What a bitch!" she thought, as soon as the door was closed. Still, she would have to speak to Léa. The girl was often rude, and if Bénédicte hadn't rescued the situation, as usual, by pretending they had to rush upstairs to study for the *baccalauréat* exam, Léa would probably have kept right at it. Things might well have become unpleasant, turning into one of those scenes with which the Gaillacs had become quite familiar since that June day in 1945 when they'd returned to Bordeaux for good and gone to get their daughter at the boarding school. Although overjoyed at the idea of leaving with her parents, Bénédicte had immediately dragged them and Sister Saint-Gabriel into the dormitory, where Léa had been lying on one of the white beds in that big empty room, sleeping with her thumb in her mouth, curled up like a fetus in its mother's womb. Billowing in the breeze, a curtain had spread out over her, then softly slipped away. When she'd opened her eyes, their utter blackness had seemed inhabited by a dark, alien presence, perceptible only to her inward gaze. It was as though the world had turned inside out for her, so that she no longer saw anything but the wrong side, rough and discolored, everywhere she looked. She had stopped talking, picked at her food with a vacant stare, and stayed wherever she was put, slumped in her chair. Her teachers no longer even tried to coax a response from her. Only Bénédicte could still get through to her, and bring a sparkle to those eyes.

What could have happened in Paris to reduce Léa to such despair? She was a difficult child, but so lively! True, she had become rather listless not long before the trip, although this might simply have been her way of coping with the uncertainty of waiting. But nothing had happened in Paris, according to Sister Saint-Gabriel. While it was always possible that Léa had been shocked by the pitiful state of those repatriated deportees in the Hôtel Lutétia, she hadn't appeared to pay much attention to them. No, no one had said anything that might have led her to suspect what had happened to her parents. Perhaps she had guessed, from what the elderly lady had said, that they might not be coming back. But she had seemed so certain of their return, that day, that Sister Saint-Gabriel had had the impression she wasn't even listening. Was there anything else? Oh yes, one small item: she'd lost a box of beads recovered that very day in the concierge's lodge at her old apartment house. She'd made a great fuss over her former plaything, but had probably realized, upon opening the box, that she was too big to string necklaces now. In any case, she had refused to go back to look for it. In fact, she'd insisted on leaving the hotel right away.

Sister Saint-Gabriel didn't quite know what to do with her. It was such a heavy responsibility. But the idea of putting her in an institution, as she'd been advised to do in Paris, was simply unacceptable. She'd become attached to the little girl, over the years. And then, she would have been running the risk of her falling back into the hands of the Jews, who were looking though all the occupied countries for their orphaned children, it was said, to send them to Palestine. Sister Saint-Gabriel had nothing against the Israelites, obviously; those poor people had more than paid for their crime against Christ. But Léa's parents had had her baptized. Even if they themselves had converted from ulterior motives, in order to protect her, she now belonged to the Roman Catholic religion. Her soul was saved, that was the essential thing. One doesn't look a gift horse in the mouth. The convent could continue to take care of her, of course. There would not be any financial difficulties. If it turned out that her parents were definitely no longer living, it would be a routine matter to have her declared a war orphan, which would entitle her to a pension sufficient to cover the expenses of her upbringing until she came of age. She would complete her primary and secondary education, and as she was quite clearly gifted, she would then have no trouble winning a university scholarship. Unless she should happen to demonstrate a religious vocation in the meantime. Misfortune often led to that, in which case the community would be only too happy to embrace her as one of its own. They were expecting the return of the mother superior any day now, and inspired by this rush of charitable feeling, Sister Saint-Gabriel, who had grown more and more animated during this monologue, declared that she would personally undertake to obtain the reverend mother's consent to this plan.

It was then that Bénédicte spoke up. She had been sitting on her friend's bed, holding her hand.

"Léa can't stay here," she said. "In the first place she has too many bad memories. And then, the other girls don't like her very much. She'd be unhappy. Even though you are very nice to her, Sister," she added hastily. "Besides, I would miss her terribly."

So saying, she looked up at her parents with those big blue eyes. It was hard to resist Bénédicte's blue eyes, not because they begged or pleaded, but because they cared so much about others, and expected so much of them, that it was painful to disappoint her.

Jean-Pierre Gaillac cleared his throat.

"Summer vacation begins in a few days," he said. "We could take Léa to our house in Saint-Palais, which wasn't touched by any of the fighting in that area. Both girls need to build up their strength, after all that distress and privation, and I'm sure they'd be better off together. When it's time for them to go back to school, we'll see. If there still hasn't been any news of Léa's parents, then we'll decide what to do."

Bénédicte turned to her friend. Léa's face had come back to life. She got up from the bed to watch in silence as Sister Marthe came and packed her meager belongings. When Bénédicte went to say goodbye to their classmates, Léa shook her head, refusing to go along. She wouldn't allow the nuns to kiss her, gave them one of her everlasting curtsies instead, and left the school without a word.

At Saint-Palais, the Gaillacs had sense enough to leave the two girls to themselves. Léa was still speaking only to Bénédicte, whom she followed like a shadow. As soon as they'd drunk their morning café au lait, they would vanish, barefoot and slender in their identical bathing suits of red and white striped cotton. For their own peace of mind, Bénédicte's parents had demanded one thing of them: that they learn how to swim. They were enrolled in a swimming club where the instructors and other children naturally took Léa for Bénédicte's little sister. After their half-hour class, the two of them played in the waves, endlessly, as though they were afraid they could never get enough of the ocean spray and foaming water—the rougher the better—to scrub their bodies clean after those grubby years of confinement. Shivering in their towels between swims, their hair streaming in the wind, their calves crusted with salt, they gathered shellfish that the scolding gulls tried to snatch away from them, and brought their prizes home triumphantly at lunchtime only to leave them rotting in a bucket on a windowsill, since no one was brave enough to cook a dozen clams and a few leathery cockles. During the obligatory nap, they returned to their imaginary world. In Léa's accounts, however, the adventures of Éric and Christian took a turn that astonished and unsettled Bénédicte: transformed into pitiless avengers, these two heroes of the Resistance shaved women's heads and invented unprecedented tortures, macabre punishments for their victims. They mutilated, shot, burned, massacred with all their might. An evil look would steal over the narrator's face. When the atmosphere became too grim and the plot twists too perverse, Bénédicte would try to tone things down, or if all else failed, interrupt the story by pretending to fall asleep. Once, just once, she attempted to find out from Léa what had happened in Paris, but gave up immediately when she saw her friend withdraw inside herself, and the light go out of her eyes.

They would spend the afternoon in long rides on their bikes, rusty old things that were too big for them, with squeaking wheels and torn seats, but the girls mastered the bikes in just a few days and rode around standing up on the pedals. They went everywhere, and everywhere they went they saw scars left by the war, since the pocket around Royan had been liberated only three months earlier, in April 1945. They found scattered sections of burned-out jeeps, an airplane wing jutting up from an abandoned clover field, gutted farms, huge bombshells that had never exploded, cartridges the girls turned over and over with their nimble little fingers and stuffed into the pockets of their shorts. Leaving their bicycles by the roadside, they would slip beneath barbed wire, carefully lifting up the strands for each other so as not to tear their blouses. On the deserted beaches, they went inside empty blockhouses carpeted with damp, chilly sand that sometimes concealed cartridge cases from machine guns. Little boys were often crawling around outside, playing war games with roughly carved wooden guns and real soldiers' helmets stuffed with rags to keep them from falling down to the boys' chins. The two girls would look on scornfully. Before fleeing, the Boches had supposedly strewn poisoned candy and booby-trapped pens about the countryside to kill the children of France. The girls looked eagerly everywhere, but never found a thing. They did, however, come across lots of tunnels and foxholes where the *maquisards* had gone to ground, and the two friends explored every last one of them. One day, in a pine forest, right in the middle of a clearing gently warmed by the sun, they discovered an entire tank, with its gun—now sheltering a bird's nest—pointing peacefully at the blue sky. Bénédicte gave a leg up to Léa, who stuck her head inside the tank, saw the dark stains and debris everywhere, and clambered down wrinkling her nose in disgust.

The Gaillacs, who knew nothing about these dangerous expeditions, were pleased to see how healthy the girls looked after two months of country living.

Bénédicte's parents had owned the house in Saint-Palais for years and knew the local farmers, from whom they obtained better food than they would have found in Bordeaux, which was still subject to restrictions. Léa and Bénédicte had gained weight and put some color back into their cheeks. In the evenings they would read a book together, nestled in one of the big leather armchairs now faded by the salt air and scuffed by the sand that had collected in its creaking seams and creases over many summers. As the girls took turns flipping the pages of their book, with their hair tumbling down on each other's shoulders and their four thickly callused feet sticking out over an armrest like jackstraws, the Gaillacs sensed that it would be impossible to separate the two friends in the fall.

Léa was behaving well, too. She never balked at the occasional request to peel vegetables, wash dishes, or trot off to the fish store for some live crabs or lobsters, and if her captives climbed the sides of the market basket, Léa stoutly snapped rubber bands around their claws, while Bénédicte hung back nervously. When the two of them set the table, Léa arranged the cutlery and glassware with fastidious precision. Although she still wasn't speaking to grown-ups very much, she was extremely polite to them, jumping up whenever they entered the room, never forgetting to end her rare communications to them with a ceremonial "monsieur" or "madame." She kept her distance, however, and shied away from physical contact. Bénédicte often snuggled against her mother, hugged her, and still liked to sit on her lap even though she was ten years old, but Léa would accept only a good-night kiss on the forehead. The two girls slept in the same room, with their windows wide open to the sea. They had pushed together the twin beds with their matching spreads of a navy blue material sprigged with white flowers. One night, seized with an irresistible longing for affection that she would ordinarily have repressed, out of instinctive delicacy toward Léa, Bénédicte called her mother and asked her to sing a lullaby, the way she used to do. After laughing gaily at her daughter for acting like a baby, the young woman sat on the edge of her bed and sang softly, in a voice that was lovely and true.

Little yellow butterflies flutter by, flutter by,
Little yellow butterflies flutter in the sky.
Little silver fishies swim round and round, round and round,
Little silver fishies swim all around the pond.
Dearest little children sleep, sleepyheads, sleepyheads,
Dearest little children sleep, tucked up in their beds.

When she had finished, she noticed that Léa, her guard down, was gazing at her trustfully. Going over to the child, she stroked her hair and said gently, "I know that you think about your mama and papa. And they think about you, too, wherever they are."

Léa's face darkened.

"I have no father or mother," she announced abruptly. "I never had any parents."

And she rolled over onto her other side.

Madame Gaillac considered herself told and never mentioned the subject again.

September was drawing to a close. Without telling the children why she was going, Madame Gaillac spent a day in Bordeaux with her husband, who no longer came out to the seashore except on weekends. He had returned to his duties as a judge, duties that had been interrupted by his voluntary departure for London during the war. Together the Gaillacs went to the boarding school to speak with Sister Saint-Gabriel and the mother superior, who had come back from Canada. No, there had been no news of Léa's parents, but they shouldn't lose hope. Even if many Jews had died, as people were saying, in those horrible concentration camps, a fair number of them must have survived. They had probably not been repatriated yet because of communication and transportation problems.

Jean-Pierre Gaillac decided at that point to tell the nuns about something he and his wife had not spoken of since their return, in part because they could not adequately describe what they had seen, and partly because they were afraid no one would believe them. They had entered the camp at Ohrdruf with a French detachment in the wake of the American army and had been present during the visit that General Eisenhower had organized for his troops. The general had declared that if American soldiers truly didn't know why they were fighting, as he had often been told, then they would know why from that day forward. In as few words as possible, the Gaillacs described the heaps of fleshless corpses stacked up like logs, the bunk beds crawling with lice, the gallows, the murderous forced labor, the whips, the dogs, the crematory ovens, the mass graves into which thousands of bodies were pushed by bulldozers, then covered with quicklime, and the few survivors, so exhausted that they kept on dying by the hundreds, expiring within minutes while their rescuers looked on. General Patton himself, although hardened by years of war, had slipped behind a hut to vomit after seeing all this for the first time. And Auschwitz, it was said, had been even worse: there the Jews, including children, had been exterminated by the tens of thousands, with poison gas, like vermin.

"Léa will never find her parents," Jean-Pierre finally told the appalled nuns. "I watched her this summer. She has but a single person left in the world: Bénédicte. Something inexplicable has happened to the two of them—let's call it friendship at first sight. Our daughter is the only one capable of helping her survive. All we can do is to make that possible. So we propose to let Léa live with us, to adopt her, eventually, if we can. How do you feel about this?"

Still stunned, the good sisters agreed to the plan, perhaps sensing that the child's unhappiness and the care she required were beyond the reach of ordinary charity. And they were in no position to oppose this project legally, as Sister Marthe's brother, their only link to Léa's parents, had been killed by the Germans before their flight, along with dozens of other Resistance members dragged from their prison cells. Besides, as a magistrate, and with his war record, Jean-Pierre Gaillac would have no trouble obtaining the assent of the judicial authorities.

"We won't be bringing the girls back here to you when school begins," he added, anxious to deliver the *coup de grâce* while his audience was still somewhat numb with shock. "We're profoundly grateful for everything you've done for them, Sisters, believe me, but they both need to forget, to have their lives filled with preoccupations more appropriate for their age. And for this they simply must have a change of scene. Don't worry, they'll come back to see you, but they should decide on their own when it's time for that. Until then, their environment must be as different as possible from what they've experienced up to now."

And that was how Léa came to live with the Gaillacs for good when the summer was over. They were unable to adopt her and give her their name, as they had wished, because her parents were not considered legally dead, only missing, and a death certificate could not be issued until ten years had passed, by which time the child would have almost attained her majority. In the absence of any legal guardian to whom her parents might have formally entrusted her before their departure, no one could give the Gaillacs the permission they sought. Léa would thus be a war orphan, but she would be placed in their care, as long as no member of her family should step forward. Back home in Saint-Palais, with Bénédicte looking on, Jean-Pierre and Jacqueline explained the situation to Léa and asked her if she would agree to stay with them while awaiting the hypothetical return of her parents. Léa said nothing about this reference to her family, and in contrast to Bénédicte, who was jumping with joy, she simply thanked her benefactors politely.

Both girls were enrolled in the fifth grade at the Lycée Mondenard. Léa was skipping two grades, but the nuns had affirmed that at eight years old, precocious by nature and from necessity, she was capable of working at that level. Besides, the Gaillacs and everyone else felt that Léa's studies would help ease her return to a normal life, and that it would be risky to separate her from Bénédicte, even during school hours. The girls got new clothes for school: red woolen pullovers knitted from unraveled yarn, and gray skirts, the creations of a seamstress with a genius for ferreting out cloth remnants, usually requisitioned from storekeepers who'd been arrested for collaborating. The Gaillacs even managed to find the children real leather shoes. At her own request, Léa's curls were cut short around the sides, and for once she allowed a gleam of pleasure to brighten her eyes when she felt herself freed from that heavy mane, so impossible to untangle, and saw her fluffy new hairdo in the mirror. Imitation leather was the best they could do in the way of school satchels, which were soon filled with books and papers.

That October in 1945, no one at the lycée knew anything about the two girls. Indignation stirred up by the revelation of Nazi crimes, the pangs of guilty conscience, and the prohibition against anti-Semitism earned the few Jewish girls in the school some sympathy, at least on the surface. So the name Lévy provoked no disagreeable reaction from either the teachers or the students. Besides, Bénédicte introduced Léa as her cousin to explain why they lived at the same address. Léa was accepted and would doubtless have been well liked if she hadn't repulsed every attempt at friendliness with glacial contempt. Refusing to join in what she called baby games (even though she was much younger than her classmates), she kept to herself during recess and waited, without jealousy but with disdainful indulgence, for Bénédicte's return whenever her more sociable friend felt the need to run and join a game of statues or capture the flag. Léa shone in all her subjects and considered her place at the top of the class only natural and indisputable. She absorbed everything—history, geography, arithmetic, science—with great facility, and her memory allowed her to reel off memorized lessons that were always word perfect. Her teachers noticed, however, that unlike the other girls she never asked for explanations, never seemed to wonder about anything, as though school were a different universe without the slightest connection to life, something that had to be mastered to please adults and earn their respect, but nothing that should inspire any real interest.

Bénédicte's parents had a lovely apartment on the Cours de Verdun, near the municipal park. They gave a great deal of independence to the girls, who walked to the lycée in the morning along little side streets and came home again the same way. Thursdays, on their day off from school, they often took the streetcar and wandered around the city, avoiding by tacit agreement the neighborhood around the Gare Saint-Jean and the boarding school, which they never talked about. A number of scores were still being settled in Bordeaux, during 1946, even if legal formalities were now being observed, unlike what had happened immediately after the Liberation. Many stores had been closed "for disinfection," and many buildings bore black swastikas painted by mysterious hands. Every day the newspaper *Sud-Ouest* displayed in its window those pages announcing executions, reporting on trials in progress, summarizing verdicts. Tracts calling for the arrest of collaborators were posted on trees and walls, some of them signed by "Doctor Guillotin." Léa would stop at every one, reading them from beginning to end with great relish. Bénédicte had grown used to these long halts during their walks and would wait patiently for Léa to rejoin her. She would turn around, pull a piece of chalk from her pocket, bend down, and with her black hair falling over her eyes, draw a hopscotch board on the sidewalk. Or she'd get her jump rope out of her satchel and whip through a series of red-hot-pepper jumps, counting out loud in her lilting voice. In any case, she always managed, at such times, to avoid looking at her friend and seeing the hard little smile tugging at the corners of her mouth.

When they went back to school in the fall of 1946, Léa was nine years old, and Bénédicte was eleven. They had no problems moving up to the sixth grade and continued to share top honors. They complemented each other, as the younger girl was better in history and Latin, while the older one excelled in French literature, which allowed each of them to do only half their schoolwork and to cheat on most of their classroom compositions, since they always sat side by side. The other students found the constancy of this friendship surprising and amusing. They had learned, sometimes the hard way, not to try to break this bond, and besides, it wasn't an exclusive one where Bénédicte was concerned. Once the films of Laurel and Hardy had begun making their flickering Sunday-afternoon appearance on white sheets hung up in bourgeois family living rooms, there was always a group of mischievous girls who would greet the arrival of the two friends in their twin-sister outfits on the first day of school by singing,

Him and me and me and him
We're just as close as two pins.
Him and me and me and him
We're together like Siamese twins.

The two would shrug and join the rest of the girls, with Léa remaining slightly apart. As for the teachers, they were more mistrustful of their relationship, and of their scholastic success as well, suspecting them of cheating. Léa made them uneasy. She didn't look like much, small as she was next to the others, frail and curly-haired in her school smock of little pink or blue checks, alternating every week, but her eyes—those opaque, black pools that seemed to look at people without seeing them—made the teachers feel that they would never reach her. Several tried, however, as the years went by, either out of irritation or vindictiveness, because she'd interrupted the eloquent flow of a lecture with a sarcastic remark or asked a thorny question during an ethics lesson—or out of kindness, because they sensed that something was definitely wrong with this intelligent girl. She continued to reject every effort to get close to her. Everyone thought she was sickly, because she was often absent for a day or two and her notes of explanation from home mentioned sore throats and bronchitis. No one knew that Bénédicte was composing these excuses, imitating her mother's handwriting. The fact that she herself was in school, looking the vice principal full in the face with those candid blue eyes as she handed in her forgeries, was enough to allay all suspicion.

Even Bénédicte didn't know where her friend went, off on her own like that. She hadn't ever asked about it, not since the day Léa had made her swear never to question her or reveal the secret of her absences. They had even marked the sacred nature of this oath by sealing it in blood, scratching their wrists with a penknife and rubbing the two cuts together. After school, the girls would meet halfway home by prearrangement in an abandoned shed where Léa sometimes hid her book satchel while she was cutting classes. They would arrive at the apartment hand in hand, calmly eat their afternoon snacks, polish off their homework, and lie flat on their stomachs to read one of the big volumes bound in red leather from the Gaillacs' ample library, which they were free to explore at will.

In spite of all their indulgence, Bénédicte's parents sometimes wondered about Léa. They had often been summoned to the lycée to hear that, although her schoolwork remained excellent, albeit impersonal, and although no one reproached her with anything specific, the teachers were amazed at how unsociable she was, unlike Bénédicte, who was popular and made friends easily despite her special bond with Léa. And then, Léa's whole attitude was one of insolence, even though she was almost excessively polite. She never laughed: she sneered. In the ninth grade she was suspended for two days for having publicly demolished, with exceptional spitefulness, the fine composition written by one of her classmates on Paul Éluard's poem, "La liberté," and read aloud by the French teacher. Commenting on the student's impassioned evocation of the nobility of the French people who had risen as one to drive the cruel Occupation forces from their native soil, for example, Léa had remarked, "It's funny, but when Monseigneur Feltin celebrated his Te Deum in the cathedral in September of '44—you remember, Bénédicte, the nuns dragged us there, and everyone gave him an ovation—well, I saw the same faces there as the year before, at the ceremony in honor of Joan of Arc with Maréchal Pétain. So they're the ones, the people who rose up en masse to boot the occupiers out of France, as our classmate says?"

Jean-Pierre Gaillac couldn't help wincing when he heard that story. The war was something Léa never mentioned at home. She still wasn't very talkative, at least not with him and his wife. Jacqueline had pointed out to him that the girl's exquisite manners masked a certain arrogance, and that she still ignored their repeated invitations to use their first names or to call them "aunt" and "uncle," stubbornly continuing even after several years to address them as "madame" and "monsieur." Jacqueline had noticed, among other things, that Léa tried whenever possible to avoid saying "please" or "thank you," using periphrases instead, and very elegantly turned ones, too. She also continued giving them only the most perfunctory of kisses. What could account for this coldness, when Léa even seemed happy to be living with them? The war had made her an orphan, true, but she was hardly the only one!

The Gaillacs often talked about all this between themselves, and sometimes with Bénédicte, without pressing her too hard, because they didn't want her to feel they were asking her to betray her friend. Their daughter had no explanation to offer, saying that she thought Léa was perfectly normal. Every now and then, however, when the Gaillacs looked into those lifeless eyes, they felt brushed by the unspeakable memory of what they had seen in Ohrdruf, and they reminded themselves that Léa had not lost her parents under ordinary circumstances. But the child couldn't know about that horror. They had protected her from everything during the years right after the war, when the truth had come out: they had hidden newspapers, turned off the radio whenever she appeared, forbidden their friends to breathe a word of it in front of her. And now, as 1950 rolled around, you hardly heard a thing anymore about what had happened to the Jews during the war. Even the Jews preferred to let the matter drop, apparently. No, Léa couldn't possibly know anything about it.

CHAPTER VIII

They were wrong. Léa knew all about it. Or at least all she'd been able to learn since the end of the war. In August of 1945, in Saint-Palais, she'd begun listening to the radio, even though she had been forbidden to touch it. The Gaillacs slept late when they were on vacation. The years of boarding school and the nighttime air raids had trained the girls to sleep lightly and wake up early. At six-fifteen on the dot, they both opened their eyes. After a glance at her friend, Bénédicte would roll over and stick her head underneath her pillow. Léa would get up, put on her bathrobe and slippers, and steal down the creaky stairs, one hand on the railing, the other holding up the thick blue plush folds of her robe, which had been cut, like Bénédicte's, from an old blackout curtain. At that hour, the steps were visible in the faint glimmer filtering through the fanlight, but Léa knew her way so well that she could have found it in complete darkness even with both hands tucked in her pockets.

She would push open the pebbled-glass door to the little room, strictly off-limits to children, where the big radio sat in splendor. Léa was small enough to huddle in the space between the perpetually damp wall and the armrest of the battered brown couch of worn corduroy. Turning on the radio, she would glue her ear to one of the two speakers—its circular outline faintly discernible behind a screen of what looked like yellow raffia—and adjust the volume as low as possible. She solved the problem of the luminous screen, which might have given her away, by covering it with her handkerchief after setting the dial on the Programme National, which broadcast the first news of the day at half past six.

That was how she followed the trial that ended with a death sentence handed down to the old Maréchal, who was immediately pardoned. At eight years old, she didn't understand everything, but she noticed that although much was said about dealings with the enemy, treason, and the humiliation inflicted upon France, the fate of those referred to as "racial deportees" was never mentioned. It was the same for Laval's trial, which took place shortly afterward, in October, and which she again followed secretly in Bordeaux, listening at different times, depending on whether Bénédicte's parents were around or not, and when they got up in the morning and went to bed. It was quite late on the evening of the fifteenth, after they'd gone upstairs for the night, and only after she'd waited a long time in the dark before daring to sneak down for the last newscast, that Léa was able to savor a young reporter's laconic announcement: "At twelve thirty-nine, Laval paid the final penalty." That night, in a frenzy of joy, she stuck a chicken feather carefully saved from the previous Sunday's dinner into her hair and danced around the shadowy living room furniture like a Sioux Indian, muttering incantations.

This man, who had been revived after his attempted suicide and sent to the firing squad wearing a tricolor sash across his white vest, had still claimed only a few days earlier that foreign Jews—like Léa's parents—had been sacrificed to save French Israelites. The latter, however, had quickly been deprived of their nationality and turned back into ordinary Jews, complete with the yellow star. Jews? Israelites? Léa didn't know what those words meant and to tell the truth, she didn't care. Right after they'd left the boarding school, she'd told Bénédicte that she didn't believe in God, because there couldn't be an almighty God mean and stupid enough to create men simply in order to exterminate them. Bénédicte had accepted this reasoning without argument. Her parents weren't church-goers. For her as well, the catechism lessons, the endless Masses in the frigid chapel, the papery host placed on the tip of one's tongue and absolutely not to be chewed on pain of instant death (but the two girls had done it a hundred times, with pounding hearts at first, then as a routine provocation)—all that belonged to a sordid and unreal past.

Bénédicte covered for these sessions with the radio as she

did for everything else. In Saint-Palais, when her parents would go off to the seaside café to enjoy once again their ritual cocktail hour, inviting the girls along for a lemonade, Bénédicte would accept while Léa declined, to no one's surprise, since she kept herself so stubbornly aloof. When it was time to go home and fix dinner, Bénédicte would frisk about, running on ahead of the grown-ups, dancing backward to rejoin them, then rushing off singing at the top of her lungs so that her parents would grow used to her antics, which allowed her to dash into the house ahead of them to warn her friend. In Bordeaux, keeping a lookout was easy because the apartment was empty all afternoon. Jean-Pierre Gaillac worked late, while his wife—who had become interested in the Communist Party when she joined the Resistance—was off at political meetings, and the cleaning woman only came in the mornings. No doors were locked, so Léa had complete access to the living room and its radio, which was newer than the one in Saint-Palais. When you raised its cover, you could see a record player and a picture of a dog, his ear cocked, listening to "His Master's Voice" on a phonograph.

One Monday at four o'clock in the afternoon during Christmas vacation in 1945, she discovered a program called "Bulletin Board for Prisoners and Deportees" that was rebroadcast at night and that she preferred to listen to later, half asleep in the darkness. For fifteen long minutes, an impassive voice would read lists of names into the silence, pausing lengthily after each sentence. With your ear right up against the loudspeaker, you could even hear regular breathing and the rustle of pages being turned. "Paul Weil is looking for his wife Emma and their children Hélène, eleven, Max, ten, Françoise, seven, Albert, two, who left Drancy in November '42 . . . Élise and Jeanne Ackerman would like to meet anyone able to give them news of their parents, who disappeared in July and October '43 . . . André is searching for his comrade Jacques, who was being treated for dysentery in the infirmary after the liberation of Buchenwald . . ." During each pause, the names fluttered painfully away, like moths that could barely move their wings, and were sucked into an endless void. Léa let herself be swallowed up by this other world that had engulfed and drowned all those living, breathing people. She listened to this silence that would linger during the pauses, then shake itself as though flinging off raindrops when strains of chamber music signaled the end of the program. If Léa had been listening since the very first broadcast, would she have one day heard the anonymous voice say in that monotone, "Léa Lévy, eight years old, is looking for her parents, last seen at the camp in Mérignac in November '42"? The Gaillacs might very well have taken such a step on their own. She never bothered to ask them such a useless question.

Léa got caught only once, in Saint-Palais, in September 1947, during the trial of Xavier Vallat, the First Minister of Jewish Affairs, which she was following with keen interest at a time when Bénédicte was in bed with the flu and unable to stand guard. When the grown-ups came into the living room unexpectedly, Léa barely had time to change stations. Blushing furiously, she admitted with downcast eyes that she sometimes gave in to temptation and listened in secret to her favorite radio series, *Sarn*, which was broadcast at that hour on another program relayed by a local transmitter. Rather relieved to find her taking an interest in something, and even to find that the ten-year-old had a tiny romantic streak, her guardians forgave her.

The year before, in fact, they'd been astonished when she returned silent and unmoved from her first real movie. For Bénédicte's eleventh birthday, her mother had taken the two girls to *Gone with the Wind*, the legendary film the French had been waiting impatiently to see. Before its official premiere, some American officers had held a few screenings for special guests in a private club in the city. Having already seen it herself at a previous showing, Madame Gaillac had dropped the girls off at the club and returned for them after the show, expecting enthusiastic chatter about Vivien Leigh's flirtatiousness, Clark Gable's dashing manner, and the dress of green velvet whipped up from a set of drapes. Sure enough, Bénédicte's eyes had been red, probably from weeping over Melanie's death. Léa had not been crying, however, and she hadn't said one word. Jacqueline Gaillac assumed Léa had been distressed by the scenes of war, by all the dead and wounded, and she reproached herself for having exposed the child to images that had perhaps brought back cruel memories.

But Léa hadn't seen any of the burning of Atlanta—although it had been much more spectacular, in technicolor, than the bombing raids on Bordeaux—because before the film, for the edification of these handpicked spectators, the Americans had shown a documentary on the camps. There was the Soviet Army, discovering the gas chambers and crematory ovens of Auschwitz in January 1945. Later, at Bergen-Belsen, a young English soldier, weeping and holding a handkerchief over his nose and mouth, drove the bulldozer that shoved thousands of emaciated corpses into a pit. The wasted bodies tumbled slowly over one another in postures like grotesque couplings. Flies clustered on the staring eyes, while dirt filled the gaping mouths. In the Little Camp at Buchenwald, the dead lay in jumbled heaps on the bunk beds inside the blocks. In Mauthausen, two detainees supported a third one, a bag of bones that would have collapsed like matchsticks without its envelope of skin. When the girls got home, Léa went straight to their room without even asking to be excused from dinner. Turning to face Bénédicte, who had run up after her, she slowly clawed scratches in her cheeks with her nails. Bénédicte tried to put her arms around her. Léa stiffened, then gently freed herself, and lying flat on her stomach, she slipped under her bed, where she stayed all night long. That evening, Bénédicte came close to admitting to her parents that her protégée's problems were beyond the therapeutic skills of her eleven years, but faithful to her promise, she did not. She made excuses for Léa, claiming she had been upset by the film, and babbled bravely all through the meal about Scarlett's run-ins with her corset and her black mammy.

From that day on, Léa's silence and her obsession grew steadily worse. Bénédicte did all she could to draw Léa out, but she felt so unnerved by the haunted look in her friend's eyes that she restrained her own natural gaiety when they were together. She tried to interest Léa in something besides that endless parade of tortured shadows her friend never stopped seeking in books, movies, newspapers, and radio programs. On Sundays, the two girls often went to the flea market on the Place Mériadeck, where one could find piles of old magazines and secondhand books among the chipped basins, rickety armchairs, and tarnished silver. Bénédicte would hunt for novels to supplement her parents' library at home. She became a voracious reader as she was growing up, and in a few years went from the sentimental stories of Hector Malot and *Little Lord Fauntleroy* to Alexander Dumas and Victor Hugo, then on to the Brontë sisters, whom she worshipped. Léa read constantly, too, out of friendship, through habit, but without love. Only one character earned her respect: the dark and brooding Heathcliff of *Wuthering Heights*, who came back as an adult to wreak suitable vengeance on the second Catherine. Léa ferreted out old copies of *Point de Vue, Objectif, Action, Le Magazine de France*, which had devoted special issues to Nazi crimes. She collected their yellowed pages and hid them beneath the drawer liners of the chest in the bedroom she shared with Bénédicte. Emaciated figures lay sprawled on gray blankets. Skeletons exploded in charnel houses set on fire with flamethrowers. Half-charred bodies were heaped up on funeral pyres. Acres of human hair, mountains of teeth, all mapped out in detail, waited in frozen expectation of an unimaginable fate. One day Léa came across an eyewitness account published in 1945, probably the first one written by a survivor of a women's concentration camp, and she practically forced it on Bénédicte. Thinking that she might better be able to help her suffering friend if she herself were to experience some of the same pain, Bénédicte agreed to read the book.

The author, a young woman of about twenty with a thoroughly French name, described with unsophisticated simplicity her activities in the Resistance, her detention in Fresnes, a prison outside Paris, and the sixteen months she spent in Ravensbrück. The two readers did not reach the same conclusion.

"It's positive proof," insisted Léa, "that everything they say is true. People were butchered like animals in these camps, starved, tortured, gassed, burned in crematory ovens. She wrote this three months after she came back. She couldn't have lied. And now everyone's forgetting. They don't want to hear about it. It's 1948, the war's only been over for three years, and even the Jews aren't thinking about anything but the creation of the state of Israel. They don't care at all about their people who disappeared. And the French care even less."

"The author cares," replied Bénédicte. "And she's not the only one. Remember those boys at the Lycée Montaigne, close to our boarding school—they were barely older than I am now. I'm thirteen. One of them was fifteen. They gave their lives for the Resistance. My parents risked theirs, too."

"Not for the Jews," hissed Léa furiously. "Oh no, not for the Jews."

She answered with such rage and conviction that Bénédicte was shaken. Sometimes she wondered how their friendship managed to survive this gap between them. They had such different outlooks on life! Bénédicte's parents often talked about politics, and from their discussions—in which she was free to join—their daughter concluded that every wrong could be righted, every evil easily challenged through reason and altruism. Weren't they themselves the proof of this? In June of 1940, they had immediately understood where the good of the nation lay and had acted accordingly. If all the French had done as they had and rallied to the side of General de Gaulle instead of backing the old Maréchal, the Boches would have quickly been chased from France, and Léa would never have been orphaned. To avoid such tragedies in the future, one had simply to be vigilant and prepared to sacrifice one's life, like those lycée students in Bordeaux and elsewhere. Bénédicte wouldn't hesitate to do so, if necessary. In the meantime, one could try to forget the war, and above all, be willing to like most people one has just met instead of instantly suspecting them, as Léa did, of Nazism or anti-Semitism. Yet though life and morality seemed clear and uncomplicated to Bénédicte, she could still understand that things weren't the same for Léa, who had lost everything because of a bunch of cowards and idiots. Besides, Léa was two years younger than she was, and while they received the same good grades in school, her friend wasn't yet capable of the same sound judgment. When Bénédicte turned her blue gaze upon Léa—a gaze that had the property of beautifying everyone it beheld—she saw once again the exhausted little ghost that had returned from Paris in May of '45, and she told herself that by loving her, she would some day be able to show her how wonderful life was.

But even Bénédicte didn't know that the paper lining their clothes drawers concealed more than newspaper articles about the Nuremberg trials or detailed reports of the medical experiments of Josef Mengele in Block 10 of the Stammlager at Auschwitz. Léa kept a much more personal account of her private vendettas. In her still-childish handwriting, she recorded in a series of spiral notebooks—with an implacable precision achieved through marginal alterations, erasures, additions, strips of paper glued on in an almost Proustian abundance—all the cases of collaboration tried in Bordeaux since the end of the war, with their outcomes: acquittals, guilty verdicts, prison terms, and often, as the years went by, death sentences. In 1950, for her thirteenth birthday, she asked for a four-color ballpoint pen, which didn't seem like much of a present to the Gaillacs, but which Léa welcomed with a most unusual twinkle of joy in her eye, to the great pleasure of her astonished guardians. This pen made Léa's record-keeping much easier, because the colored pencils she'd been using until then didn't work very well with calligraphy. Now she was able to retrace in red ink the capital letters and exclamation points calling attention to the entry in the 1948 notebook announcing the conferring of the Legion of Honor on the Prefect of Constantine, the former Secretary General of the Prefecture of Gironde, Maurice Papon.

For a long time she had tried to find a way to attend these "purification" trials in person, out of a desire for revenge, first of all, and also because of something she'd heard while eavesdropping on Bénédicte's parents shortly after her arrival in Saint-Palais. From their conversation she'd learned why she hadn't been arrested with her father and mother, thus escaping the fate of the two hundred and twenty-six Jewish children shipped out of Bordeaux during the Occupation, almost all of whom were exterminated in Auschwitz-Birkenau. This scene of her rescue, forgotten along with everything else and which she'd never managed to recall, was what she hoped to relive one day by recognizing her would-be captors among the handcuffed defendants in court. Then she would truly know everything, because if seeing them provoked the anticipated effect, she would make them talk, even if she had to wait until she was old enough to torture them herself.

But how could a little girl sneak into a military tribunal? The one in Bordeaux was on the Rue de Pessac, in a former barracks on the southern outskirts of the city, far from her apartment and her lycée. She cut classes several times to reconnoiter the area. Getting there turned out to be fairly easy: all she had to do was take the number 9 or 10 streetcar at the Barrière Saint-Médard and get off about ten minutes later at the Barrière de Pessac. It took her no more than half an hour, walking included. At first she didn't dare get too close, and stayed hidden behind a tree. Then, on her fourth or fifth visit, she saw a fat woman wearing a plaid coat and a headscarf rooting around nervously in her shopping basket for her papers, to show them to the guard on duty at the gate. Three little kids were clustered around her, and on impulse, Léa ran over to join them. The mother was too preoccupied to notice a thing, and when she finally found her papers, Léa trooped through the door in her wake.

That day she realized that being only twelve, and looking two years younger, was not so much a problem as a blessing. On her next visit, to make the most of this unexpected asset, she brought along her book satchel instead of leaving it in the shed where she met Bénédicte after school. And taking full advantage of the opportunities offered by a military tribunal sitting in judgment on civilians, she usually managed to slip inside with one family, then find another one to sit next to in the courtroom.

After a few weeks, afraid of being found out, she boldly staked everything on another, riskier ploy: she sat right down on the first step of the dais where the judges' table stood. It was a Thursday, but she'd kept on her blue-and-white checked school smock. She pulled a textbook and some paper from her satchel and began to suck thoughtfully on her pen. Unlike everyone else, she did not rise at the entrance of the magistrates, one of whom, the public prosecutor, almost tripped over her.

"What do you think you're doing?" he asked Léa in surprise.

"I'm the cloakroom lady's daughter," she replied. "Mama told me to wait in here. She doesn't want me wandering around out in the street or to be bored at home alone. And I have to do my homework someplace . . ."

"Well, don't stay here on this platform," said the embarrassed official. "Why don't you go sit down in that corner over there? You can do your homework on your lap."

And so, as the years went by, the scrawny schoolgirl—to whom no one paid any attention as she grew into a skinny adolescent—became a fixture of the tribunal. Since Léa was careful to attend the sessions only at irregular intervals, no one questioned her identity or noticed that the cloakroom lady had been succeeded by a second one, and a third, while her supposed daughter was still around. The prosecutor who had unwittingly promoted her deception began by winking at her during his solemn entry into the courtroom and wound up patting her on the head as he left. One evening when he returned to get a file he had forgotten, he asked her nicely if she received good grades in school and whether all the noise and hubbub of the trials didn't make it hard for her to do her homework. When she had the nerve to whine in reply that she didn't understand math at all, he had her come up onto the dais, where he sat comfortably at the long table in the empty courtroom to explain a geometry problem to her. Seeing her chance, she walked out to the courtyard with him, holding his hand, so as to be noticed by the guard at the gate, who from then on let her come and go as she pleased and passed the word on to the other guards. The solicitude of the prominent personage who had elected himself her protector and even her private tutor put an absolute end to whatever doubts might have occurred to any subordinate officials.

Actually, Léa hardly touched her homework during the court sessions. It was the spiral notebooks that filled up, with names she thought no one would ever decipher, since she wrote them in the childish alphabet perfected years before with Bénédicte. To represent the guilty verdicts, she used a code inspired by a game her classmates played in a completely different spirit and setting: hangman. Unfortunately, the tiny figure dangling from his gallows was completed less and less frequently now. There was a procession of collaborators, profiteers, and informers, but the time was past when women's heads were shaved, and men with signs saying "Traitor" hanging around their necks were tied to the closest tree by an angry crowd and shot. Lawyers were appealing for mercy from the court, pointing out the defendant's age, his straitened circumstances, his family responsibilities, and they always managed to dig up some Resistance member he'd helped out or a Jew he'd tipped off the night before a roundup. The stiffest sentences were commuted, amnesty laws were in the wind, and "purification" was no longer the order of the day. Léa drew in the left foot of a hanged man one last time on June 2, 1953, and she drew it in all the more gleefully because it marked a double execution. On that day, after three years of appeals, on the very site of the camp at Mérignac, a firing squad dispatched a man who had taken part in the atrocities of August 1944 and another who had worked for the Division of Jewish Affairs. After a moment's thought, she made the bodies green, the color of hope, and enclosed them in a black box.

CHAPTER IX

She didn't make this ceremonial gesture while sitting in the courtroom, however. She had been *persona non grata* there for almost a month. She'd had high hopes for a trial that had begun in late April, in particular because it would be her last chance to recognize those two policemen from so long ago. Léa had been quite careful not to attend the tribunal too often, but now she needed a serious alibi in order to follow the entire trial, which was to run at least one week beyond her school's Easter vacation. This time she had a lot of trouble getting help from Bénédicte, whose worried misgivings were turning to exasperation and remorse and who finally agreed to her plan only if Léa promised this would be her last escapade. Léa gave her word all the more readily since the French militiamen involved in the massacre at Oradour-sur-Glane* had already been sentenced three months earlier—sentenced with the utmost lenience, moreover, and pardoned immediately—and this upcoming trial was the last one scheduled at the tribunal.

So the lycée administration was officially informed that Léa was suffering from scarlet fever, a dreadful disease requiring the strictest quarantine. Since Bénédicte had already had scarlet fever as a small child, no one was surprised that she wasn't afraid of catching it, and every morning, while satchels were clicked shut and notebooks plopped noisily down onto desks, she handed over to the teacher all the homework the supposed convalescent was completing as brilliantly as usual. When teachers solemnly questioned her solicitously about her friend's condition, Bénédicte would answer them without batting an eye before heading back to her seat, expertly dodging

---

*Translator's note: The German SS burned this village near Limoges to the ground, killing 642 men, women, and children.

spitballs flicked her way by girls who were jealous of the success their youngest classmate enjoyed without even taking the trouble to come to school.

Léa passed the first part of her *baccalauréat* with distinction. She was supposed to have completed it at home (by special dispensation) under the same conditions as everyone else, but she casually tossed it off with the enthusiastic assistance of the prosecutor, who thought he was helping her study some questions from previous exams. To explain why she wouldn't be coming to the courtroom anymore later on, Léa told him some story about a worrisome reaction to a TB skin test that would require her to rest, and quite probably, she added with a brave little smile, spend some time in an observation sanatorium after she had taken her "bac" exam. She also asked him for permission to formally attend the trial in session when she had finished her homework. After eight years of delays, the court was judging members of the Kommandos des Sicherheitspolizei und des Sicherheitsdienstes, the KDS in Bordeaux—chief organizers of all measures taken against the Resistance and the Jews in the entire southwest region. Given that she was sixteen years old and about to complete her *baccalauréat*, she told the prosecutor, she could only benefit from witnessing this historic occasion. Besides, she hoped to begin studying law the following year, and her recent interest in this vocation had been inspired by her eminent protector. What better source of practical experience could she find, she insisted, coughing weakly to finish softening him up.

He was easily persuaded to find her a seat in one of the front rows. The preliminary investigation of this case had been dragging on for so many years that in the meantime most of the accused, and in particular their French collaborators, had simply vanished or had the charges against them dismissed. Léa stared intently at the three prisoners who remained. The two most important ones were former SS officers, now dressed in double-breasted suits and ties. One of them seemed to her like the classic handsome blond Aryan, an athletic butcher from a race of slaughterers, while the other, a smaller, darker, balding man, looked like a typical model bureaucrat, so used to following orders that on the instructions of his superiors he would toss a dead rat or a live baby into a boiler with perfect indifference. The accused faced serious charges: brutality, torture, the execution of hostages, and of course, the deportation of Jews. Léa didn't miss one word of the terrible accusations brought against them, which could only lead to death sentences she was already anticipating with pleasure. But when the defense began to refute the charges and call its witnesses, the trial took a turn that had become only too familiar. The torturers had shown admirable restraint during their interrogations; they were not responsible for the selection of the hostages to be shot, or for the deportations, since their orders had come from Paris. They had saved members of the Resistance, had spared human lives. At worst, they had behaved like soldiers, only regretfully carrying out their painful duty. Witnesses for the defense paraded before the court: policemen, shopkeepers, even a survivor of the camps. As the days went by, Léa, who had listened triumphantly at first, now began to slump in her seat, pale with anger. Those men were directly responsible for her parents' death! On May fifth, the verdict was returned: a few years in prison, covered by the time spent in detention awaiting trial. As of the following day, they would be free men.

It was just after the sentence had been pronounced and when the lawyers were turning around to congratulate their clients that Léa jumped up and scrambled over the benches, pushing aside everyone in her way. When her pink skirt caught on a nail, she tore it loose without even a glance at the damage and burst into the center aisle with the ripped material hanging down around her ankle socks. Hands on hips, she planted herself in front of the defendants, who could not help recoiling from this Fury whose big black eyes had dark circles under them, and whose shock of hair as frizzy as a black girl's curled around a Peter Pan collar edged with white scalloped braid. She was so small and flat-chested that she didn't seem more than thirteen years old, but she threw out that chest so defiantly that she popped a button off her blouse.

"Hey! You!" she yelled with all her might. "What did you do with my mother and father?"

The accusation echoed around the crowded courtroom like divine thunder over Mount Sinai. Then a deathly silence fell. Finally everyone returned to life as the lawyers in their gowns protested with great flapping of their long sleeves, the spectators shouted out questions and interjections, two policemen appeared on either side of Léa, and the prosecutor ordered the bailiff to clear the room.

When it was quiet again, the baffled man tried to coax some kind of explanation from his protégée, who remained silent even when he threatened to charge her with contempt of court and assuming a false identity. In the end he had to search her book satchel to find her name and address. And discovered that the supposed daughter of the cloakroom lady lived in one of the most fashionable neighborhoods of Bordeaux, between the Allées de Tourny and Les Chartrons, in a former mansion converted into apartments overlooking the lawns and lake of the municipal park. Despite her famished air, she probably gorged herself on brioches and hot chocolate at the elegant Pâtisserie Jegher and laughed at the modest treats he'd brought her from time to time to plump her up a little. Realizing that she'd been fooling him for years, he insisted nevertheless on taking her home himself, hoping to fathom the mystery of her behavior and wishing, out of lingering affection, to spare her from being escorted to her door by policemen—who would doubtless have found the journey a lot more unpleasant for themselves than for her. Not a single word was spoken during the entire trip.

At the apartment on the Cours de Verdun, Léa went straight to her room. As for Jean-Pierre Gaillac, who had just arrived home from work, he was dumbfounded to learn from one of his colleagues—a magistrate whose rank was equal to his own and whom he knew slightly, even though he himself had always refused to have anything to do with the "purification" trials—what kind of secret activities his ward had been up to since she was twelve years old. He was especially incensed by the story about the sanatorium and by all the wheedling and flattery the heartless minx had used for so long to hoodwink this elderly bachelor, who was still so affected by it that before leaving, he begged Jean-Pierre not to be too hard on the culprit. Two things were clear: Léa was a shameless liar, and Bénédicte had clearly helped—if not encouraged—her in this deception. His first impulse was to summon both girls and reproach the one for her ingratitude and duplicity, the other for her foolishness and lies, then cap his sermon with a suitably impressive punishment. In any case, they would be confined to the apartment, at least until the *baccalauréat*. It was only after a great effort at self-control that he decided to wait for his wife's return and let the girls stew in their own anxiety for a few hours.

Jacqueline Gaillac was not as surprised as her husband had been to learn of Léa's exploits. She was quiet for a long moment before expressing an opinion rather different from his own.

"This is all our fault," she said. "We haven't paid enough attention to this child."

"But we surrounded her with affection!" protested Jean-Pierre. "We kept everything away from her, all the details about the mass murder that claimed her parents . . ."

"Well," his wife broke in, "we were probably wrong. By taking all those precautions, we must have forced her to discover the truth on her own. Listen, I think we should talk to Bénédicte first, without Léa. She may have been tricking us for years, but I don't think she's very good at lying. She's the only one who can explain to us what we haven't been able to see. And after all the uproar Léa just caused, we'd better let her calm down before we speak with her. It'll make things a little easier . . ."

Bénédicte came in hanging her head, and even though her

parents spoke gently to her, at their first question she burst into tears—crying from relief, her mother shrewdly realized, even more than from remorse. Her daughter must have worried terribly about Léa, and if she covered up for her friend, it could only be through mistakes in judgment that she had surely come to regret later on without being able to put an end to them. This constant anguish had been a wretched burden.

"Why didn't you ever tell us anything?"

Bénédicte looked up at her mother with eyes so pale they seemed to have lost all color.

"I swore not to," she stammered, adding, as though this childish excuse were the only reasonable explanation for her behavior, "we sealed the pact in blood."

"But that's kid stuff!" exclaimed her father. "Léa was in terrible danger. She has to be sick to have acted the way she did. You kept us from realizing it, so we didn't give her the help she needed. Do you understand how serious this is? And while we're at it, you'd better tell us everything. She must have done more than this. What other strange behavior has she been up to that you've hidden from us?"

"Well, sometimes she scares me. She'll scratch her face. Whenever you noticed it, we told you she'd been clawed by a cat. She spends hours hiding under her bed or beneath a table. One day . . ."

"One day?" prompted her mother.

"One day she sat on the windowsill with her legs outside, and she stayed there a long time. She was really pale. She wouldn't say anything. I had a lot of trouble getting her to come back inside."

"What else?"

"She swallowed a bottle of aspirin, about a year ago. But she wasn't even sick."

"But Bénédicte!" exclaimed her father in exasperation. "You're eighteen years old now! Even if it was understandable for you to give in to Léa when you were children, you must know that there's something wrong with her. How could you have hidden all this from us?"

Bénédicte began to cry again.

"She was so cheerful when she was little," she sobbed, as soon as she could manage to speak again. "So funny. So pink and chubby. So sure her parents were going to come back. By the time you met her, she'd already changed. And then she began to despair. I just couldn't betray her."

"But what could have made her lose hope like that?" asked Jacqueline.

Her daughter hesitated.

"I think it was the pictures."

"Pictures?"

"Léa collects articles about the camps. Our chest of drawers is full of them. Magazines from '46,'47 . . . With awful pictures."

Now it was her parents' turn to grow pale. They thought they could imagine only too well the effect those photos had had on Léa when she was nine or ten. And they were wrong again.

"She doesn't talk to me about them anymore," continued Bénédicte. "But once she told me something I've never forgotten. She said that all those bones dumped like that, into those mass graves—that there wasn't anything human about them. And that since her body should have been there too, she wasn't human either."

"All right," said Jean-Pierre slowly, after a long silence. "If I understand correctly, she knows everything. She's read the articles, probably heard things on the radio, seen documentaries at the movies, perhaps. She's followed all these trials, listened to these collaborators give their cynical excuses. And all this has had such an effect on her that she can't get on with her life. Don't cry, Bénédicte. None of this is your fault. Léa was so cold, so polite, so irreproachable. I admit I thought she was insensitive. I believed she'd forgotten her parents, or at least that she wasn't tortured by their memory. Your mother often warned me about that. I didn't listen to her. Go get Léa. And don't worry. We won't yell at her."

Bénédicte was gone for a long time, probably confessing that she'd broken her promise. At last she reappeared, dragging with her a grim and white-faced Léa who hadn't even changed out of her torn dress.

"Léa," said Jacqueline as gently as she could, "we must apologize to you."

Léa's look of bitter hatred wavered in surprise.

"For all these years we've thought that you'd forgotten your parents, that you didn't miss them, that you never knew what happened to them. You still love them very much, don't you?"

"No, I hate them!" shrieked Léa, and then she began sobbing, too.

"You hate them! But why?"

"Because they abandoned me . . ."

"Calm down. And sit down. You can't really believe that. They saved you. You have no idea how much love it took for them to give you up to a complete stranger."

Léa recoiled, and with the reflex of a hunted animal, turned instinctively toward the door. Bénédicte put her arms around her friend's shoulders and led her over to a big armchair, where she made her sit down. Standing behind her, with both hands on the back of the chair, she leaned over, resting her forehead on Léa's hair.

"Try to talk," she murmured. "We can't go on like this, you know that. We're not children anymore. The blood bond, the secret alphabets, Éric and Christian—that was over a long time ago. You have to let go of all that. Face up to things. Explain."

Léa twisted around to gaze feverishly into her friend's face. She shuddered violently, and ran her tongue over her lips.

"The way they acted was stupid, and cowardly," she said finally, choking out the words. "They had money. They could have left the country in time, gone to America."

"It wasn't that easy."

"Others did it. But no—they had faith in France, I suppose."

"Léa, the French people weren't all bastards during the war."

"There were you two, of course, and others in the Resistance, and the boys at the Lycée Montaigne Bénédicte's always telling me about. But if I were to ask you, would you dare tell me that all that bravery was meant to save people like my parents?"

Jean-Pierre and Jacqueline looked at each other. Once again, Léa had hit home.

"We didn't know, Léa. Almost no one knew. We only found out in '45, when the camps were liberated. There were rumors, I admit, but we never imagined the scope of the disaster or its circumstances. You're right, we did fight to save French honor, to liberate France, more than to protect the Jews. But we did fight. And we weren't the only ones who ran risks. Think about the sisters who hid you at your boarding school, for example."

"Oh, they weren't worried," replied Léa harshly. "They probably figured no one would ever shoot nuns."

"Don't be ridiculous. A great many nuns were arrested and shot or deported, and priests, too. They must have known that. Listen, we can't change your mind about everything tonight. What's important is for the two of you to be set free from all this. What you put Bénédicte through was very hard for her to bear, even if her pain doesn't begin to compare with yours. You're aware of that?"

Léa's bold front collapsed again.

"I'm really sorry I made Bénédicte tell lies and write fake medical excuses and change the notes our teachers sent to you. I hope you've forgiven her."

True to her nature, however, she couldn't help adding, "But I'm not sorry for anything else."

The social repercussions of this scandal in the courtroom proved as harmful to the two girls as the family confrontation at home was healing and cathartic. The disruption at the tribunal could not pass unnoticed by the upper echelons of Bordeaux society. The main problem was a scholastic one. It was May: the second part of the *baccalauréat* was coming up soon. It was vital to explain things to the principal of Mondenard, who was certainly not going to appreciate having been deceived. The Gaillacs and the two girls made an appointment with her. Her reply was blunt. Léa and Bénédicte were the best students in their class. They were more than likely to pass their exams "with distinction," which would show to advantage in the lycée's records. Therefore, they would be allowed to attend classes until July. After which, no matter how well they did on the *baccalauréat*, they could consider themselves expelled.

The girls disappointed their principal by receiving only a "satisfactory." Still, this result was enough to ensure their admission to Lettres Supérieures at the Lycée Fénelon in Paris, where they would be taking classes to begin preparing for the entrance exam to the École Normale Supérieure. The Gaillacs had finally arrived at this solution after much thought and many late-night discussions with Bénédicte and Léa—who, for the first time since they had taken her into their home, seemed to speak frankly to them. Staying in Bordeaux was unthinkable. Neither the girls nor the parents could go downtown anymore without the old maids at their tables in the Pâtisserie Jegher or Darricau's burying their noses in their whipped cream and darting sidelong glances at them from beady little eyes. That, my dear Jenny, they would whisper, snobbier than ever in their ringlets, is what happens when a couple from a perfectly good background insists on taking in a stray from who knows where, surely from some central European ghetto constantly spreading the kinds of problems that prevent decent Frenchmen from getting along by themselves. And that, Maggie dear, is the sort of mess you end up in by flirting too shamelessly with a Communist Party that still claims one quarter of the votes in Bordeaux (on the pretext that they lost seventy-five thousand killed during the war), thus preventing the city from recovering its former prosperous serenity. The

Gaillacs and their ward were lucky they weren't blamed for the terrible forest fire of 1949 that had ravaged the Landes and even threatened the suburbs of Bordeaux, or the Colorado beetles that kept invading the potato fields, or the myxomatosis that was killing the rabbits before hunters could have the pleasure of shooting them, or the epidemic of hoof-and-mouth disease that was decimating the flocks, or the interruption of shipments from the French West Indies that had halted the delivery of rum to the storehouses on the Chartrons docks (rebuilt at great expense), or the phylloxera from which the vineyards of Médoc had suffered so heavily. Stalin's death in March had seemed like a partial consolation. In June, when the Rosenbergs were electrocuted, the former Pétainists who had gone over to the Gaullist Chaban-Delmas had the satisfaction of concluding definitively that they'd been right about that, at least, all along.

This didn't prevent the Gaillacs from celebrating with champagne in Saint-Palais at the end of July, after the girls had passed the bac. It was a very mild summer, and it was to be their last in the ornate old villa, because its fussy balconies, crumbling cornices, and lopsided gables were slated for demolition. The region was slowly rising from its ashes. Reminders of the fighting were disappearing one by one, and only the indestructible blockhouses still poked their snouts up over the dunes, awash in the sand that refused to bury them.

Léa remained taciturn, but was no longer silent, and the Gaillacs began to hope she might get well again. They felt that after all those years, she was beginning to accept the idea that she was a member—albeit a distant one—of the family. Eager to take advantage of this development, they hardly let their rambunctious teenagers out of their sight all summer long.

In August, the entire country was paralyzed by strikes. No one could get in or out of Saint-Palais anymore because there were no trains or gasoline. In that little seaside resort town where the shops were forced to close, one after the other, and where people used candles for light after dark, everyone seemed condemned to do the same thing over and over, more and more slowly, throughout all eternity. Time seemed to have stood still. Parents and children got out their rusty old bikes and took long rides, wearing shorts and shirts over their perpetually damp bathing suits. They went off to swim and toss a ball around away from the summer visitors, where the vast beach of the Grande Côte stretched out by the ocean for them alone. They strolled along the woodland paths shaded by evergreen oaks in the Forêt de La Palmyre and picnicked in the sunshine on a carpet of pine needles, or went all the way to La Tremblade to dine beside the oyster beds, devouring plates of oysters and enormous slices of bread and salted butter washed down with white wine. They went to the Ile d'Oléron by ferry, the only public transportation still in operation, and their wheezy bikes clattered along roads lined with mimosas and rose laurels. Sometimes they went down the coast to the coves of Saint-Georges-de-Didonne or Meschers and spent whole afternoons reading and gorging themselves on warm shrimps purchased from itinerant vendors on the docks.

In the evening, the Gaillacs would return to their little house that was not long for this world and have cocktails in the garden, on lounge chairs. The adults would talk politics; the Laniel government—that beefy dictatorship, as the novelist François Mauriac put it—would be forced to give in to the strikers' anger sooner or later, and then Pierre Mendès France would take power, extract the country from that Indo-Chinese quagmire, defuse the situation in Morocco, and recognize the right of all peoples to self-determination. Justice would triumph, as it always did when people were willing to fight for it. Bénédicte and Léa would listen, the one with enthusiasm, the other with skeptical reserve.

Stars would come out in the darkening sky as a crisp little breeze blew in off the ocean, rustling the branches of the stone pines, stirring up scents of blossoms and salt spray. Bats zigzagged among the trees. Conversation would languish. In the silence, they could hear a split beam creak or a chunk of stone from a wall drop into a flower bed. They would sigh and go in to dinner, but never without one or the other of the adults thinking back nostalgically to their own youth and commenting hopefully on the bright and studious future in store for the two girls come October, off in the Latin Quarter.

CHAPTER X

"So you're Jewish, mademoiselle?"

"No," replied Léa coldly.

The friendly black face grew round with surprise.

"Your name is Lévy and you're not Jewish?"

"No."

The hand raising the freshly filled pipe to the waiting mouth now fell back again. Why had he bothered finally striking up a conversation with this skinny kid who always sat all alone in her corner, idly stirring her spoon around in an empty coffee cup and daydreaming over an open book? Really, these French were just impossible for an American to understand. Serious novelist that he was, he'd been interested in her for a few weeks now. No matter what the weather, she would bundle up in a big black sweater that hung down to her thighs and a gray skirt that drooped well below her knees. There were often runs in her stockings. She wasn't much to look at, with that pale, sharp little face overwhelmed by a mass of frizzy curls. He'd spoken to her in the hope of learning something about her, and also out of kindness, because she seemed so alone and so lost without the friend who always accompanied her or inevitably showed up in the end. You'd have thought those two girls lived in that bistro and spent their lives talking. They never seemed to have any problem finding something to chat about, as though they hadn't seen each other for years, when they actually lived together in an apartment in that very building—he'd learned this from the *patronne*. The girl had looked up at him with a veiled gaze, as though her dark eyes were covered with an opaque film that made her blind to other people; she'd answered him politely, telling him her name, and now she was telling him off with that flagrant lie, that idiotic denial. From cowardice? Stupidity? Fear of an anti-Semitic remark, even though the war had been over for almost ten years?

The arrival of her friend saved him from having to explain that he of all people—a black man driven from his own country by McCarthyism, a Negro whom the Ku Klux Klan would have loved to lynch—could hardly be suspected of anti-Semitism. The older girl seemed so much healthier than her friend, so blooming with her lovely fair complexion, her short black hair, and her big blue eyes that beamed affectionately at you, as though she didn't even need to know you to like you. And she didn't hide her hips and breasts under a baggy old existentialist uniform. He smiled back at her and raised his eyebrows in Léa's direction, with an expression of amused bafflement.

Bénédicte pulled in her stomach to slip between the edge of the brown Formica table and the banquette of torn red imitation leather. For an instant her backside—displayed to advantage by a plaid wool skirt and a particularly flattering wide black patent leather belt—hovered within arm's reach; the American sighed and buried his nose again in his newspaper. Bénédicte sat down and briskly flipped over the cover of the book lying open by Léa's coffee cup.

"Ah, you're reading Sartre. *Reflections on the Jewish Question*. Interesting?"

Léa nodded.

"Instructive. I'm beginning to understand why the goyim didn't let the Final Solution run its course. It's because the anti-Semite has a vital need for the Jew, to justify his own failures. Without the Jews, he'd have no one to blame but himself or his own kind. You'd have revolutions breaking out everywhere."

"Which reminds me, did you attend that meeting of the Jewish Students Union like you were going to?"

"No. Sartre also says one is a Jew only through the gaze of the Other and that one can simply decide not to be Jewish. I've decided that I'm not."

Listening behind the screen of his newspaper, the writer couldn't help smiling once again. When that kid reached the final pages of her book, she'd find a quotation from him (which she wouldn't attribute to him, however, because she didn't know his name): "There is no black problem in America. There is only a white problem."

"So, are you coming with me to sign up for the Communist Youth League?"

"Oh, if you want."

"You don't seem too thrilled about it."

"Sure I am. It just seems to me that your Communists ought to clean up their own mess before lecturing everyone else. Haven't you read that Stalinist defector, Kravtchenko?"

"That's a set-up, everyone says so, even your precious Sartre."

"But they still exist, right, the Soviet concentration camps? They don't bother you? Well, if you want to prance around shouting 'U.S. go home!' I'll keep you company."

"Can't make an omelet without breaking some eggs," replied Bénédicte primly.

With her fingernail, she carefully tore open the end of a pack of Gauloises and tapped out a cigarette. Before flicking open her fake lizard Silvermatch lighter, she examined the cigarette, pulling out a tiny splinter of wood that she dropped into the already overflowing ashtray. Then she lit up, inhaled deeply, and leaned back against the banquette, lazily contemplating the crowd of regulars who filled the bistro from ten in the morning until quite late at night. Near the entrance, next to the pinball machine, were the old gamblers, who lined up their stacks of poker chips on a round tray decorated with Dubonnet advertisements or rolled their dice and piled up their matches on the green cloth they brought for games of 421. Near by, a young man in glasses was hunched over a sea of closely written pages rippling with tiny letters. Across from Bénédicte, behind the bar, the waiter was indolently polishing the glassware set out below the rows of bottles. The *patronne*, a corpulent woman with thick black hair gathered into a large chignon, was sitting ramrod straight on her chair over in the corner where cigarettes were sold. Facing the entrance was the American, waiting for his compatriots to arrive. There was no one all the way in the back: customers only used those tables if they had secrets to tell or if they were in love and couldn't wait any longer to begin kissing. The back tables remained unclaimed because they were too close to the swinging doors on the Turkish toilet, from which an impressive stench escaped whenever anyone went in or out, but every group of regulars—card players, intellectuals, writers, black musicians—had its time-honored spot in the Café Le Tournon.

Bénédicte ordered a *café crème* and some bread and butter. Arnold, the resident German shepherd, sidled hopefully over. Léa gave him her usual kick under the table. He retreated a few inches and plopped down on his haunches, keeping an eye on the sugar cubes arrayed along the saucer's edge. This rather stupid animal—whom everyone fussed over, buttering up his owner in case of dire financial need—just couldn't get it through his head that someone might loathe him. With what he believed was a touching air, he raised his muzzle toward the hideous mural (doubtless painted under duress by an impoverished artist to pay off his debt) that covered an entire wall with the green lawns and bilious yellow walks of the nearby Jardin du Luxembourg, with its statues, its splashing fountains and basins, and its lovers.

This bistro, located practically next door to the Sénat, was the reason why Léa and Bénédicte's stay in Paris turned out to be less studious than had been anticipated. And when Jean-Pierre Gaillac had noticed the establishment on the ground floor of the building in which the girls would be living, in two rooms an elderly cousin was only too happy to rent out, he had made a face—to the great amusement of his wife, who had gleefully reminded him of his own youthful follies: hadn't they met in a bistro near the Panthéon, where he'd been vilifying the French bourgeoisie in endless fiery harangues instead of attending classes in law school? Besides, they had to wrench Léa free from the vicious circle of her obsessions. That was the only reason why they were letting the two girls go off on their own for the time being. Didn't that make the risk worthwhile? Jean-Pierre hadn't seemed impressed by the argument, but he had been reassured to see that the Jardin du Luxembourg was so close by. The girls would surely prefer to breathe good fresh air instead of the cigarette smoke that filled the bistro at all hours, day or night. And anyway, their studies would keep them so busy that they wouldn't have time to hang around in cafés. At noon, they'd eat lunch in the cafeteria of the lycée. In the evening, their landlady would let them use her kitchen. During vacations, they would naturally come back to Bordeaux.

The beginning of the school year of 1953-54 seemed to prove him right. Léa and Bénédicte approached Paris as cautiously as a cat circling its saucer, testing the contents with tiny licks from a careful tongue. They found the grimy walls of the Lycée Fénelon less pleasing than the creamy stone façade of the Lycée Mondenard, with its tall windows framed in rose brick overlooking the flowered terraces of Bordeaux's shopping streets. And their new classmates—most of whom were also from the provinces—turned out to be real bookworms who'd gotten ahead thanks to private tutoring and sleepless nights of study, and they were fiercely determined to win admission to the prestigious École Normale Supérieure de Sèvres. As Léa, perched on a stove, brandished a gilt-paper laurel crown above the head of her friend, who was swathed in a sheet, Bénédicte gamely delivered the Latin speech they had concocted for their initiation ritual, but the performance drew only scornful reviews. The first Greek composition they threw together in their usual offhand manner lost forty points in the first ten lines (the rest weren't even corrected) and showed them that their teachers meant business as well. On the horizon loomed the two exams—one at Christmas, the other at Easter—that would decide who graduated to the second-year class preparing to compete for entrance to the École Normale Supérieure, and in that field of starters, the first-year students thought only of checking out the competition and drawing ahead of their rivals. The second-year girls, called "squares," despised the younger ones—and the third-year students, or "cubes," looked down on the squares. This climate of frantic competition clashed with Bénédicte's egalitarian ideas and provoked sarcastic comments from Léa, who wondered out loud how people going on twenty years old could be so infantile. The *Vara tibi cagna*, the hymn the students weren't allowed to sing until their second year (if they passed, that is), and the folklore surrounding the song did not seem worth that desperate effort to beat out everyone else in the class. The rather unlikely prospect of someday getting into a *grande école* and winding up in a student body as unlikeable, in a word, as those mean little peasants in the boarding school in Bordeaux offered nothing to compensate for at least three years of hard labor.

So it was only during the first two trimesters that Léa and Bénédicte set their alarm clock for seven each weekday morning, trotted down the Rue de Tournon, crossed the Boulevard Saint-Germain, and took the Rue de l'Éperon to their first-year prep classes at the Lycée Fénelon. On the way back, they sometimes made a detour via the Boul'Mich and gazed longingly at movie posters or the welcoming terraces of the cafés that flanked the venerable Panthéon. But Bénédicte had been put in charge, and she was determined, this time, to assume her responsibilities more conscientiously and with greater maturity than she had in the past. She still wondered, and with some dismay, how she could ever have lied for so long to her trusting parents and behaved so childishly in her relationship with Léa. Walking by Saint-Sulpice, looking in the display window of the Alsatia bookstore with its blowups of book covers from the *Signposts* series, which now had many more titles, she'd remarked to Léa that Éric and Christian looked like Nazi jerks right out of the Hitler Youth. Still off in the clouds, Léa had not even recognized them.

One evening in the third trimester, however, the idea of returning to the dark apartment of their elderly landlady and shouting as they did every day into the trembling hand cupped around an ear that yes, things were fine at school and no, they didn't need anything, and then tackling Malebranche's *Dialogues*, the subject of their next composition, made Bénédicte's heart sink. "Why don't we have a cup of coffee here before we go upstairs to work?" she'd suggested outside the Café Le Tournon. The door was propped open to let in the fresh spring breeze. The sawdust on the tile floor squeaked beneath their shoes. The table in the left rear corner became miraculously free at their entrance. They sat down there with no inkling that this table would be their home away from home for the next two years and that everyone would tacitly recognize their claim to it. The friendly atmosphere in the bistro, the snatches of political conversations they heard without daring to join in themselves, the black customers who never seemed to agree about anything, constantly squabbling and feuding with one another, and who seemed just as ready to start singing "We Shall Overcome" with upraised fists as they were to push back the tables and dance a breathtaking boogie-woogie—all this thrilled Bénédicte from the very first moment. This was real life! Here, among these people arguing their heads off and grabbing newspapers out of one another's hands, not in a lycée where fuddy-duddy teachers who'd never heard of any philosophers after Bergson spent their time pounding the ablative absolute into the ambitious heads of prematurely aged grinds! By unspoken agreement, this spur-of-the-moment visit became a daily habit. The next afternoon, the girls had only to glance at each other before heading into the café, over to the *patronne* to buy their first pack of Gauloises, and off to take possession of their table, which they found waiting for them. Besides, the advantage of the courses they were taking was that they were so much more difficult than a first year over at the Sorbonne that you could easily pass the final exams in arts or science there, and with distinction, too. Which they did, correctly figuring that with this success in hand, it would be easier to explain to Bénédicte's parents over the summer vacation that the École Normale Supérieure could do without them very nicely, and vice versa.

Once again, the discussion back home in Bordeaux was a spirited one. Léa and Bénédicte were certainly as pale as papier-mâché, at least in the opinion of Jean-Pierre, who soon made his daughter confess that they were eating more hot dogs than steaks. But that wasn't anything that couldn't be remedied by a diet rich in milk, good red meat, and green vegetables. Luckily, food shortages were a thing of the past. Of course, the girls were smoking, too, and that first Gauloise after dinner had its little effect. But Bénédicte was going on nineteen, and Léa had just turned seventeen, so the grownups—both heavy smokers—could hardly take exception to that. The plan to switch over to the Sorbonne to begin studying for a bachelor of arts degree, on the other hand, was something they needed to talk over. Weren't the girls exaggerating a bit when they compared preparing for the École Normale Supérieure to being stuck in a reform school, and described Sèvres as a penitentiary? Wasn't the École one of those places where the mind comes into its own, and wasn't the example of a graduate like Simone de Beauvoir enough to inspire them?

Jacqueline Gaillac kept quiet. She had no trouble understanding how after so many years, a lycée, even in Paris, can seem like a prison. She also suspected, gazing fondly at her daughter, who was talking away, holding her cigarette jauntily between two slender fingers, that the idea of spending another two or three years in an all-female environment, even one enlivened by the secret visits of the boys from the École Normale Supérieure on the Rue d'Ulm, was a singularly unattractive prospect. Jean-Pierre as well must have sensed that boys were involved in this somehow because he dug in his heels, staring at Bénédicte in a kind of stupor as they argued. It seemed to him that her eyelashes were longer, her lips redder, and that her breasts were now swelling beneath the close-fitting bodice of her dress when just three months earlier they'd been as flat as two fried eggs. The discussion took so long that he fetched a bottle of cognac and poured himself a glass. The next thing he knew, the girls were holding out their glasses, too. He gave them each a drop, which they tossed off with alarming ease.

"And anyway," said Léa, whose wan cheeks were a bit flushed from the brandy, "you can see how studying Greek, and Latin, and some ancient philosophers just isn't enough for us when there's so much going on now. Mendès France ending the war in Indochina the way you were hoping he would last year, that's great. But what about Morocco, Algeria, the social injustice closer to home? Look at that priest, the Abbé Pierre, who launched his appeal on behalf of the homeless last February. You simply can't leave the poor to Catholic charity alone. Bénédicte and I want to do our share. We joined the Communist Youth League," she added proudly.

Bénédicte shot her friend a sidelong glance. She was always staggered by Léa's slyness and her colossal nerve, but this time it was all for a good cause. As for her father, he was reflecting, as he pulled on his brand-new beard, that he'd never heard Léa go on at such length before—and about something that had nothing to do with her own personal problems. So, Léa was opening up, getting involved in political issues. Perhaps she was finally realizing that the whole world hadn't died with the Jews in Auschwitz, that the war had been over for ten years but that other wars were brewing—that they'd just narrowly escaped one, in fact—and that the struggle to spare mankind from the horrors of such conflagrations was never-ending. If she'd learned this lesson, then he and his wife had won, and Léa was cured.

He looked inquiringly at Jacqueline. She'd been studying the girls, too. In the pool of light cast by the dining room chandelier onto the stained and rumpled tablecloth, dirty dishes, and overflowing ashtrays attesting to the length and liveliness of the discussion, Bénédicte looked radiant. Encouraged by her father's attitude, for she could clearly see that he was weakening, she had impulsively begun an impassioned apology of Parisian life. Both girls had seen plays staged by Jean Vilar in the resonant cathedral of the Théâtre National Populaire. Two thousand people, almost all of them from the working classes, had given a standing ovation to that theatrical company performing out there on a bare stage, the only décor a quartet of trees the actors themselves shifted around between acts! Such fervor, such energy—he had no idea! And one day—he wasn't going to believe this—on their way home along the Rue de Tournon, they'd passed the same guy, in cords and a sweater, that they'd seen the previous evening wearing the white costume of Kleist's Prince de Hombourg! He lived right next door! She'd gone into ecstasies at the sight of him, and Léa had had to tug her by the sleeve several times to rouse her from her trance. And even their building was famous. The Austrian novelist Joseph Roth had lived there. Every day the girls encountered film directors, intellectuals who'd come out of the Resistance—the cofounder of the publishing house Éditions de Minuit, for example—and musicians, too, and black writers fighting for civil rights. One writer, a short, really ugly man, kept saying he intended to set America on fire! Only a last-minute reflex of caution prevented Bénédicte from blurting out exactly where they were meeting all these people.

Next to her friend's glowing vitality, glossy black hair, and those sparkling blue eyes, Léa's pale little face seemed almost ghostly now that her brief show of impassioned feeling was over. Looking at her, Jacqueline Gaillac had a frightening intuition. That child with the ashen complexion, who looked so hollow-eyed in the bright flame of the cigarette lighter, suddenly seemed to her no more than Bénédicte's shadow. As though Léa needed the light shining from her friend to leave her own faint imprint on this earth. Or even as though she were already dead, and had been for a long, long time, ever since 1945, perhaps, and had only been kept artificially alive by the older girl's energy and life force. Jacqueline suddenly remembered something she'd so often heard said about this girl: "No one has any idea where she comes from." And for the first time, she saw that Léa was obviously a stranger in these familiar surroundings where she should have seemed naturally at home after ten years. She looked like a scraggly weed sprung from nowhere in a well-organized garden planted with brilliantly colorful blooms. This child really knew nothing at all about herself, either about her origins or her identity. She was no more than scorched earth, a landscape of ashes, enclosed in the shifting boundaries of a human form by the magnetic force emanating from Bénédicte. Jacqueline caught her breath in fear and pity. What would happen to the girl when she was separated from her friend in time, as she inevitably would be?

"Léa," she said, interrupting Bénédicte's animated political conversation with her father, "Léa, listen. Are you sure you want to get an arts degree? What if you studied Russian, instead? I would have liked you to learn it at the Lycée Mondenard, but they didn't have a teacher. You could start studying it at the Sorbonne."

"Russian?" asked Léa. "Why?"

"Because it's the language your parents spoke. Because I've always thought that one day you might want to go over there to see if you can find out whether you have any family left, and that might be possible, now that the prospect of another war seems to be fading."

"The Russians have nothing to do with me," replied Léa. "Bénédicte's my family. And you two, of course."

"One doesn't exclude the other. You never felt drawn towards their literature, their culture?"

"No, never. Dostoyevsky drives me up a wall and Tolstoy bores me stiff. They have nothing to do with me," she repeated.

"She's not Russian and she has also decided that she's not Jewish," broke in Bénédicte gaily. "After all, it's better that way. Nationalism is a reactionary idea, you've told us a hundred times. The revolution will be international or it won't be at all. And it'll be easier to bring about with someone who isn't tied down to any country or religion," she added, wrapping her arm affectionately around Léa's shoulders. "An elf, a pure soul and a free spirit, who'll drag me away from life's temptations when I get too tangled up in them, and help me ascend to the rarefied heights of perfect Communism!"

Jean-Pierre burst out laughing. Jacqueline forced herself to smile, but the image of Léa's face—turned toward Bénédicte to drink in her words, as though eager to soak up her radiance—would return to haunt her a few years later.

CHAPTER XI

Lying prone on her bed, propped up on her elbows and peering into a tiny mirror set right in front of her nose, Bénédicte was making one last desperate attempt to put on some false eyelashes. She had shortened them (reluctantly), evened them off (more or less) with a tiny pair of scissors, curled them with a clamp that looked like an instrument of torture, applied the special glue, and now she was trying to stick them on, but the outside corners kept poking up and tickling her eyebrows. And besides, she was crying from having to keep her eyes wide open, which wasn't helping things. Yet it had all seemed so simple. She wriggled her bare toes in frustration. And the sardonic looks she was getting from Léa, who was sprawled in an armchair pretending to read *Being and Nothingness*, were driving her even crazier.

"Why don't you put on a different record?" she suggested, to distract Léa.

Reaching behind her armchair, Léa moved the tone arm back to the outer grooves of the record that had been going silently around and around on the turntable. The worn-out needle scratched and spat before settling into the placid chords of Brassens's bawdy "Watch Out for the Gorilla," which they must have listened to a hundred times because it was banned on the radio.

Giving up on the false eyelashes, since she'd run out of glue, Bénédicte put on an old pair of gloves so her nails wouldn't start a run in her nylons, which she fastened to a garter belt with rather tired elastic straps, checking afterward to see if the seams were straight in back. She draped a chiffon scarf over her head to keep her dark foundation makeup from staining the pink gingham dress she slipped on: it had buttons down the back, and a full skirt puffed out by a crinoline as stiff as cardboard. She'd applied thick strokes of black eyeliner and extended them toward her temples, giving herself the incongruous appearance of a blue-eyed Egyptian. Wincing, she maneuvered her feet into white pumps with spike heels. Then she draped a cardigan, also white, around her shoulders and fastened only the top button. She put the finishing touch on her handiwork by knotting a little headscarf under her chin.

"How do I look?" she asked, after taking doubtful stock of her reflection in the mirror on the wardrobe that took up half the space in the small room.

"Fine," replied Léa tersely.

Bénédicte went closer to the mirror and inspected her eyelids.

"Do you think I ought to take some of this stuff off?"

"Why bother? Just make sure you're always in profile, of course, like the bas-reliefs in the Louvre. And speak only in hieroglyphics, and give your date a Rosetta stone so he can figure out what you're saying."

Bénédicte shrugged, but smiled all the same.

"Would you do something for me?" she asked, trying to scrape off the excess eyeliner without smudging the edges.

"I've already guessed what."

At twenty, Bénédicte fell in love every week, usually with someone who turned out to be unsuitable (because he was too old for her and seeking favors she had no intention of granting to anyone before marriage) or else disappointing (because he was politically immature, a knee-jerk anti-Communist, a petty bourgeois reluctant to get involved, or an out-and-out fascist). She used the Café Le Tournon for all her rendezvous, but because she was so unsure of herself she always sent Léa down beforehand to scout around and bring back a report on that week's candidate. Was he there? If so, alone or with others? Was he reading? Reading what? How was he dressed? Wearing a tie, or with his collar unbuttoned? What was he drinking? Coffee, beer, or lemonade? Did he seem nervous, anxious at being kept waiting, glancing frequently at the door? But most important of all, had he taken a seat right in the middle of the bistro or at one of those back tables, the selection of which augured well for the possibility of a flirtation, albeit a malodorous one?

"It's only six," observed Léa. "You told him to come at seven, so I'd be surprised if he were here already. But are you seriously going to march in a demonstration in that getup?"

Bénédicte smacked her forehead in exasperation, then grabbed a bag into which she stuffed a pair of low-heeled shoes, some slacks, and a sweater.

"You're right, I'll change in the car or in the ladies' room at the theater. We're going to leave for Grenoble right after *Mother Courage*. You're sure you don't want to come along with us? Antoine likes you a lot, you know," she added generously. "He loves to argue with you. He says you have an analytical mind and enough political savvy to see through all the imperialist lies."

"No, thanks. Nice of you to invite me, but I don't want to miss Jankélévitch's course at the Sorbonne tomorrow. I have a question to ask him."

With expert solicitude, Bénédicte glanced at her friend to gauge her mood. Léa had been doing better for a while now. There was an occasional glimmer of life in that dark gaze. She was reading a great deal, even though she hardly ever looked at the books recommended by the Party. She attended political meetings, although without much conviction—and without forgoing the satisfaction of lobbing the odd bombshell into the proceedings, either, and provoking the invariable response.

"You're going down to Grenoble to lie on the railroad tracks to keep soldiers from leaving for Algeria. Fine. But when your student deferments are cancelled and it comes time to choose between going to Algeria or going to prison, do you know what you'll do?"

Followed by the weary reply.

"The Party will decide, comrade."

Or else:

"You jeer at cops who rip 'The Deserter' out of neighborhood jukeboxes, you fight fascist gangs with bicycle chains, and you whimper, I might add, when we disinfect your glorious wounds with hydrogen peroxide. But when the Communist deputies voted to give full powers to the Guy Mollet government two months ago, I didn't hear you protesting. So it's the Hitler-Stalin pact all over again?"

"Stop carping, comrade. You're acting as though you'd never heard of democratic centralism. When the Party decides, we decide, that's all."

Only Léa's Jewish name kept her from being expelled—that plus the fact that everyone knew her parents had perished in the death camps. She was perfectly aware of this and seemed intent on seeing just how far she could push that guilty conscience protecting her. "Being an alibi instead of a scapegoat—I find that rather refreshing," she told Bénédicte, who simply rolled her eyes.

Bénédicte loved to dance, and whenever she could she dragged her friend along to little nightclubs, where Léa was content merely to observe. She would park herself on a bar stool with a Coca-Cola or a gin fizz, depending on the state of her finances, and solemnly watch Bénédicte go by, her black hair flying as she whirled around the floor with a natural grace and sense of rhythm that had would-be partners lining up to dance with her.

Léa herself had quickly given up on these boys who would snap their fingers impatiently, grabbing her wrist to pull her out into the dancing without even turning to look at her, because they couldn't take their eyes off Bénédicte. Stiff as a stick, Léa was never invited twice. Bénédicte had tried a hundred times to teach her the steps, but whenever she urged her to join in, Léa replied quite honestly that she just didn't understand the music.

Whenever their joint cash reserves were low, however, she was perfectly willing to help replenish them by accompanying Bénédicte into the bistro's kitchen. There, by standing arrangement with the *patronne,* who would have preferred them to work as hostesses but accepted them as scullery maids, the two girls fished leftover veal scallops out of the garbage, pieced them together with egg whites, slathered them with bread crumbs, and served them with big smiles to fresh customers. Léa had taken particular pleasure, one night, in placing two such doctored plates before the poet Louis Aragon and Elsa Triolet, whom she claimed, for reasons known only to herself, to find unbearable.

So, things were looking rather promising to Bénédicte, who was delighted to see Léa starting to lead a normal life. Bénédicte naturally felt that her mother's fears about Léa were unfounded, yet strangely enough, these fears only grew worse. Jacqueline spoke of them to her daughter on every possible occasion, as though Léa were a jalopy in poor condition whose defects required immediate repair after years of dangerous neglect. According to Jacqueline, her ward was lacking just about everything she needed to be truly rooted in the human condition: a father to rebel against (or not), a mother with whom to identify (or not), brothers, sisters, uncles, aunts, cousins, grandparents, someone who would at least share certain characteristics and attitudes with her, a family likeness, or in the absence of such individuals themselves, then at the very least, memories and mementos, documents, photos, and on and on—a birthplace, a language, a culture, even an ancestral cemetery, this militant leftist went on to say, quoting the arch-conservative Maurice Barrès. She often asked a puzzling question, which Bénédicte never remembered to pass on to Léa because it seemed so unimportant: why had she been so happy to have her hair cut when she was eight, only to let it grow long again two years later? Why, in spite of all suggestions to the contrary, did she keep her face hidden behind that frizzy mop? Yes, why? And why not? Jacqueline was also afraid that Léa might become too much of a burden for her daughter. But she was wrong. Léa was both very light and quite heavy, thought Bénédicte, a bit like those specks of anti-matter that pop up in science-fiction novels. Friendship made her feather-light. Yet her presence evoked so many memories of pain and fear that she weighed Bénédicte down. There was one thing, though, that particularly bothered Bénédicte.

While she was getting ready to go off to Grenoble, she finally dared to ask the question that had been nagging at her for months.

"Why don't you ever fall in love, too, once in a while? You just turned nineteen. You're not going to spend your whole life with your nose in a book. If you ever deigned to show an interest in someone, we could double-date! Wouldn't that be nicer?"

"Not interested," replied Léa. "And anyway, boys don't like me, you know that."

Bénédicte's searching gaze softened as she considered her friend's scrawny figure.

"I've been meaning to talk to you about that," she said smoothly. "Don't you think it could be because you haven't started your periods yet? I mean, that's not really normal, at your age."

Léa turned around to move the tone arm back to the beginning of the record.

"Sure it is. Your mother took me to see a doctor about it, remember? He said it wasn't anything unusual and would sort itself out in the end."

"You were fourteen years old then! And you've never been willing to go back there. If you want, I'll make an appointment for you."

"We'll see," said Léa. "Considering the fact that you writhe around in pain on your bed every month, holding your stomach, I think I'm better off the way I am."

The two girls were going to be getting their bachelor's degrees in arts without ever having set foot in the Sorbonne—or only rarely—that entire year. Their field of study was a triangle linking the Café Le Tournon to the Champollion movie theater, where they were making up for lost time in the film department, and the little club on the Rue des Canettes where they ended their evenings after the bistro closed. It wasn't that they hadn't tried. Duly registered at the end of the summer in 1954, they'd shown up regularly at first, in the huge lecture rooms with walls and ceilings crawling with dusty gilt moldings, and benches that had begun the school year packed only to empty out in the same season and the same rhythm as the trees shedding their leaves in the Jardin du Luxembourg. After a couple of weeks, the few students who still came to sit in front of the rostrum and try to catch a word or two of the lectures read for the tenth straight year by a drowsy old professor were priests and nuns, motivated by their sense of duty, or by their superiors. Léa and Bénédicte quickly realized that the ever-popular sets of duplicated notes were a godsend and that for a small sum, they could purchase the precise contents of the lectures mumbled by the doddering dyspeptics, which left plenty of time to perfect their cinematic education, attend meetings of the Communist Youth League, and spend a good part of their nights dancing.

If Léa did actually go to the Sorbonne every week during the school year of 1955–56, it was because something entirely unforeseen had happened. One day when she was on her way to the registrar's office with a paper that had been missing—for quite a long time—from her file, she heard an explosion of laughter behind the closed door of a lecture room as she was passing by out in the hall. Not only was this an exotic sound in such surroundings, but the sign on the door indicated that the philosophy students within were attending a class in ethics. Laughter? During an ethics lecture? Unable to believe her ears, Léa opened the door and found a room so full of young people that some of them had given up trying to squeeze onto the crowded benches and were sitting in the aisles or leaning against the walls. The merriment had just died away, as abruptly as it had begun. Standing on the dais was a thin little man with a sharp profile; a thick lock of fair hair flopped over his aquiline nose. He held a piece of paper as tiny as a cigarette wrapper, and in a breathless voice so husky it seemed close to tears, he was explaining a concept he called the Almost-nothing to an audience hanging on his every word. Fascinated, Léa edged closer. "Anything," he whispered into a silence in which his low voice was perfectly audible, "anything is better than misunderstanding! Anything—including outright warfare!"

That was how Léa learned of the existence of Vladimir Jankélévitch. The very next day, she dashed off to the library to find out what he had written. Although she wasn't tempted by his *Treatise on the Virtues*, she came across an article entitled "With Honor and Dignity," published in 1948. Misunderstanding took a severe beating in this text, which was a ferocious attack on Vichy France—the France of "senility" and "shame"—and an indictment of the equivocations that were hampering the purification trials: "Every scoundrel has his alibi, every collaborator has hidden his Jew in a closet or obtained some false document for a Resistance fighter! There are neither guilty nor innocent anymore, and the collaboration trials are crumbling just as the moral evidence of disgrace and betrayal is melting away."

Léa was overjoyed. This meant that when she was eleven and thought herself the only one struggling against indifference, denial, and lies, the only one refusing to write off six million people and acquit their murderers, there was at least one adult who, like her, refused to compromise. And not just any old adult: a professor at the Sorbonne! From that day on, she never missed a single one of his classes. This moralist was a Jew, like her. Perhaps being Jewish meant something, after all. Maybe the Sartrean explanation, which had seemed so straightforward and satisfying to her, fell a touch short. She read more of Jankélévitch's writings, listened to him, kept her usual mistrustful eye on him as the months went by. Could one really, without joining the ranks of either the true believers or the Zionists, imagine a voluntary Jewish identity? Could one love one's fellow man without either forgiving or forgetting? And like her, "Janké" was Russian as well. If she were to let herself be guided by him, would Dostoyevsky or Tolstoy eventually awaken in her echoes of some sense of belonging? After a great deal of thought, she made up her mind: she would get her bachelor of arts degree and begin studying philosophy next year, even without Bénédicte, if she couldn't convince her to do the same thing. She decided to talk to "Janké" after class the next day.

"Are you going downstairs or not?" asked Bénédicte.

Léa returned from the bistro with good news: Antoine had arrived. She rather liked Antoine. He was definitely cute. Looked a little like Burt Lancaster. And Léa had found him more mature than most of the others. Gauloises. Coffee. No tie. Reading *L'Humanité*, the Communist newspaper. Sitting at one of the back tables, but that didn't mean anything, as Bénédicte observed, since he'd never been to their café before and wasn't familiar with its customs.

"I'll let him fidget for five minutes and then I'm off," she said. "By the way, don't forget Kaled. If he needs to crash with us, he'll knock on the door—you remember the signal? Three knocks, pause, then two more. I'd be surprised if he came, he's supposed to leave France tomorrow, but if he should come by, open up right away. He's got the cops on his tail."

The members of their cell were taking turns putting up Kaled, who belonged to the Algerian Communist Party. No one knew exactly what it was he did, but they knew the police were hot on his heels, and they suspected that his high rank in the National Liberation Front put him in mortal danger. He wouldn't have been the first one, in that year of 1956, to be simply shot down in a hail of machine-gun bullets if push came to shove.

"You and your fellaheen," sighed Léa. "Let them figure it out for themselves. Some day we're going to wind up behind bars without even knowing why we sacrificed the best years of our lives. But don't worry, I'll take care of him."

Bénédicte, busily checking her eye makeup one last time in the mirror, turned around abruptly to face her friend.

"Don't say such things. You don't really think that. And we're not going to get started on those same old arguments about Algeria," she added earnestly. "I understand how much of your attitude at meetings is sheer provocation. But I'd like to point something out to you anyway . . . If you were to persist in refusing to support the National Liberation Front, you'd be making yourself an accessory to a crime. The same crime, basically, as the one the collaborators committed against you during the war."

Léa couldn't help blinking.

"I'll think about it, I swear," she replied, with the sweet smile she never gave to anyone but Bénédicte. "I just prefer Janké's doubts and hesitations to the temporary absolute certainties of the Party. We'll talk about it when you get back. In the meantime, don't worry."

"And while I'm gone, don't you go see that film about the camps, *Night and Fog*."

"I promise. I'm going to bed early, for once. I'll hit the books tomorrow morning down in the café. I'll be in class in the afternoon. Then I'll come home and listen to the radio. Maybe I'll hear news of your heroic deeds. Or you can tell me about them yourself tomorrow evening."

Bénédicte flew out the door. More or less true to her word, Léa stayed up reading longer than she'd planned, went to sleep wondering if she'd be better off trying to speak to Jankélévitch before or after his lecture, woke up at around ten, and went downstairs to have breakfast in the Café. She sat at their favorite table, where she ordered coffee and croissants, gave Arnold his ritual kick, and opened her book. The place wasn't busy yet, but the *patronne* was already sitting in state behind her cigarettes with her knitting in her lap, looking even grimmer than usual. In reply to Léa's greeting, she had simply grunted and returned immediately to her work. The clicking of her needles and the clatter of dice shaken mechanically in a cup by a solitary player were the only sounds in the sleepy bistro.

The door burst open. Léa looked up. A regular customer entered in a hurry and tossed some coins on the copper tray by the cash register.

"Did you hear the news on the radio?" he said, pocketing his Gitanes. "What a tragedy, that poor girl dying in a car accident, only twenty years old . . ."

The *patronne*'s involuntary glance at her corner table told Léa everything there was to know. She shut her book, left the café, and went back upstairs. She wandered around the room for a few minutes, putting away a pair of stockings that were lying around, playing idly with the false eyelashes Bénédicte had tossed onto the bed, putting the tone arm up on its little perch and slipping the Brassens record back into its sleeve. She stopped in front of the wardrobe mirror and calmly tore out handfuls of her hair. Then, still calmly, she scratched her face with her nails. She went to sit down under the table, curling up into a ball with her head between her knees and her arms wrapped around her legs. Hours passed, or days. Her attention was completely absorbed by a delicate ringing, like the tinkling clatter of beads dropping over her one by one, then pouring down in a cascade.

At some point, this fragile music was invaded by a banging that must have been going on for a long time. Its rhythm replaced the pattering of hail that had become a cataract inside her head. Three knocks, then two. Three, two. She heard a voice, frantic and insistent. The words were quite clear. "Bénédicte, Léa, are you there? Open up, quick! Open the door!" Kaled. Algeria. The war. The police. Must let him in. Accessory to a crime. Her hands moved up her legs, grabbed the edge of the table, gripped it hard to help her stand up, then clamped themselves over her ears. She could still hear the uproar out on the landing, though: shouts, fighting, maybe gunshots. But the shower of beads had changed to a rain of ashes, which covered her completely in a shadowy gray blanket that finally deadened all sound.